Southern Cross

Mike Sims

Southern Cross

Acknowledgements

To my family and friends that believed in me and my writing.

Also to all the readers of my work for which I am deeply thankful.

For Alfredo

Southern Cross

This novel is a work of fiction. Names, descriptions, entities, and incidents included in the story are products of the author's imagination. Any resemblance to actual persons, events, and entities is entirely coincidental. The opinions expressed by the author are not necessarily those of Mazzaroth.

Published by Mazzaroth
www.Mazzaroth.net

ISBN: 978-0-9982983-9-9
Fiction / Adventure

Contents

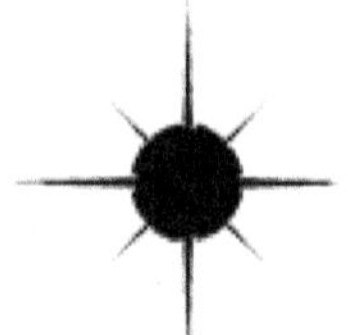

Miguel

Miguel

The distant stars seem so constant to us as we plan and scheme below them. After the sun has dominated the day, the heavens are our reassurance that despite our attempt to manage the affairs on the Earth, they are the same. They comfort us in the pitch of a black sky. While our sun gives life to all things on our planet the distant suns play their part in our lives and in nature as rhythm and signs. It is in that night air that a twelve-year-old boy name Miguel Ortiz sits on the rocks and stares at the stars as he ponders.

"The stars are near and far yet they seem to make shapes. If constellations are real then it must mean God is here with us making them so we can all see them that way," he mutters to himself.

A distant voice of his dad Manuel cries out, "Miguel! Come home!"

"Coming!" Miguel yells back as he continues to look up at the night sky. I wonder what else is up there? he thinks.

Miguel runs back home which is a small village on a plateau backdropped by distant mountains. They live in the state of Michoacán, Mexico and their little village named Las Oilas almost

a primitive community of thirty-four residents. They live a simple life with no modern appliances, no cell phones, no TV – nothing to connect them to the world as you and I know it in the 1990s. They have been there for seven generations living in an arid, desert area with no real discernable form or landmark to speak of. Even the mountains in the distant seem non-descriptive. They perform their daily tasks of growing vegetables and tending to chickens, cows, and sheep for their livelihood and food stores. One well in the center of town provides all the life-giving fluid they need. It is simple but in certain ways paradise, as no one bothers them from the outside.

Their life may be simple but they are by no means a simple-minded people. They choose a life that is debt free and unrestrained by the modernness of the world. They know that living the convenience of that life comes with a price, a price that they'd rather not have to pay, but they enjoy the true freedom of lifeless tied down. The stresses of the daily chores of their lives also acts as a stress relief as they make them strong and healthy, not weakened by a life of comfort. They do not need supplements for their food as it has all the nutrients they need. All in their lives

Miguel

has a balance. Most people in the modern world strive for that balance or at least wish for it, but time is their enemy and excuse their way. Not for the villagers. Their way is to handle the task at hand and enjoy the time to do things that most modern people wait for two weeks out of the year to do. It is a sermon lived by few and known by many. Yet for the villagers it is hard but rewarding. The rhythm of a good life plays music that grows the soul in ways not understood. Only those that are lucky enough to afford such a life can reap the benefits of the quiet song. A song that sings out enough that everyone knows it is there. This is their life and their story.

Most villagers are illiterate yet traveling teachers come to teach their young sometimes. However, some have left to find a different life in the cities. One that did is Carlos, Miguel's uncle. He went to college and work as a geologist for a local oil and gas company. He visits his old home village sometimes and brings Miguel things to entice his nephew to seek a life elsewhere. Miguel's dad is not convinced as he feels the village life is all that they need. His philosophy is embraced by those living there and look to him for leadership and steadfastness.

As Miguel arrives home, he sees his father working on a wooden contraption.

“Late again, son,” his father observes.

“Sorry, Dad. The stars make me think a lot and I lose track of time.”

“Nothing wrong with thinking but you need your sleep. You have chores during the day, you know.”

“Yes, sir.” Miguel watches his dad and asks, “What is that?”

“It is a slapper.”

Miguel laughs. “A slapper?”

Manuel joins in his laughter. “Yes, son, a slapper. You see, the goats eat everything including the food meant for the chickens. So, we put the chicken food in the basket as normal but the slapper sits above it. The chickens can eat no problem but the larger goat has to move it out of the way which makes this thing spin and hit the goat which startles them. Hopefully, it will keep them out.”

“We keep them separate though.”

“Not always, son.”

“Okay, Dad.” Miguel climbs his ladder to the shelf that acts as his bedroom while Manuel packs his project away.

“Time for me to sleep as well,” Manuel says as they both make their way to bed.

“Dad.”

Miguel

"Yes, son."

"Do you think I will be an astronomer someday?"

"I think anything is possible, but you are old enough to understand that your life is here and you will most likely be living as a farmer like me."

"Uncle made it out of here."

"This is not a jail, son. I just don't want you to be disappointed. It takes a lot of learning to be an astronomer."

"I learned how to read."

"So did I, son, but I am quite content being here."

"I *will* be an astronomer someday, Dad."

"I admire your ambition. We will see how you think in a few years' time. Now get some sleep."

Miguel rolls over and stares at the ceiling of their homemade of trees and sod. He feels overwhelmed by the prospect of being an astronomer but ever hopeful. However, he can't repress the dreadful feeling that his dad might be right. He closes his eyes to sleep feeling sad when a piece of dirt from the ceiling falls from between the wood and hits him on the head. He opens his eyes and a small hole has appeared with a star shining through to him. He smiles and stares at it until he drifts asleep.

The next morning Miguel is awakened by his dad standing on his room ladder.

"Wake up, son." Manuel sees the sun peering in through the ceiling hole. "I have some food on the table. After you eat, fix that hole above your bed. Must be a board loose on the roof." His dad climbs down the short ladder and goes to the table.

Miguel looks at the hole. "My window to the universe," he says to himself as he joins his father at the breakfast table where a corn-like concoction awaits him. Miguel chews on his dad's culinary creation and asks, "Dad, you think of mom very often?"

"Almost every day, son."

"Do you think she would have wanted me to be a farmer or an astronomer?"

Manuel slowly stirs his food in the bowl. "Eat your food," he says without answering the question.

"Yes, sir. I just wonder what she would think of me if she was still alive."

"She would be proud of you and even your star watching stuff. But I think she would tell you to be a farmer like me. You know she did not marry an astronomer but a farmer. She was pretty enough to marry anyone she wanted."

Miguel

Miguel continues to eat his food wondering about his mother. She was taken by an illness when he was four years old. He has faint memories of her holding him and singing to him. He cannot remember the words but the tune carries in his heart like a drum that beats with every moment.

The Typical Day

Miguel and his dad start the day feeding the goats, sheep, cows, and chickens. Miguel draws water from the well and pours the good bucket into the two he carries on a stick side by side using his shoulders.

"Here we go," Manuel says, grabbing a bucket. He pours the drinking trough for the animals as they come running for their nourishment. "Nothing more rewarding than taking care of animals that take care of you," he tells Miguel.

"Yes, sir."

"Come on, then. Let's move the dairy cows to the barn so the ladies can milk them."

As they finish in the barn Miguel looks over as Sarah Martinez and her daughter Laura pass them to milk the cows. Laura smiles at Miguel but, as he smiles back, she quickly sticks her tongue out at him. Miguel looks puzzled as she laughs.

"Laura, stop that," her mother says.

Miguel stares as they enter the barn and Laura stops and looks over her shoulder at Miguel.

"Laura!" her mom yells, drawing Laura into the barn.

Manuel looks at Miguel with a sense of relief that his son may be a farmer yet. “Son.” Manuel starts back to their house.

“Yes, sir,” Miguel replies, catching up with his dad.

“Laura is quite the cutie isn’t she?” Manuel says later, as he washes his hands at the sink.

“She is alright,” Miguel says noncommittally.

“If I were you, I would be chasing after that one.”

“Dad! She is eleven.”

“Oh, big age difference, son.”

“We are good friends, Dad. I can’t see her the other way.”

“Hmm. Okay.”

Manuel pulls out some bread and beans mashed up and puts them on the table. “Here you go, son.”

“Dad, do you think we can go hiking?” Miguel asks while chewing his food.

“In this heat?”

“At night and look at the stars.”

“Son, there is nothing to see.”

“I was thinking if we went to the mountains we could see the stars better.”

The Typical Day

"Do you know how far away those mountains are, son? They are just bumps in the distance which means they are way too far for us to get to."

"You think Uncle Carlos can take me the next time he visits?"

"No, it is too dangerous. There are lots of bad people out there."

Miguel looks disappointed as keeps eating. "Dad?"

Manuel drops his head. "Yes, son."

"Can we just at least hike down to the old dried river? We went there once before."

"Will it shut you up for a while?"

"Yes, sir."

Manuel looks at his son as Miguel stares back in anticipation. "Sure," he says eventually after we fix the sheep fence we will make our way out."

"Yea!"

Miguel eats his food in record time and waits for his dad to be done so they can finish the chores. It seems ages before Manuel finally finishes eating and starts to the sheep fence. There are twenty or so sheep the villagers collectively keep there. But constant moving around by the sheep and being startled by anything around them has broken part of the fence. Manuel and Miguel take branches from old oak trees and some from junipers

found in the less arid regions a little further away and cut the straightest branches to fix the fence. Miguel anxiously helps to complete the task.

"Well, son, if you only worked like that all the time, this village would have no problems," his dad observes.

"Can we go now, Dad?"

"Yes. Let's grab the water bottles."

They grab old plastic water bottles from supplies Manuel's brother left with other visiting relatives who try to bring some of the modern world to Las Oilas. Miguel is excited and runs into the house to grab the bottles and, by the time his dad has brought the tools back home, Miguel is ready.

"Okay, son, let's go." They head west toward an old dry river bed cut off after a dam was placed in a larger town for commercial farmers. The villagers had to move to tap the aquifers with a well to keep their village alive many years ago. Manuel remembers those days well as a young boy himself. But life is normal for him anyway. Once a routine is established, life becomes normal and acceptable in any condition.

After an hour's walking, they arrive at the dried river bed.

"Here it was, son. Seen enough?"

The Typical Day

"Little further, Dad."

"Why? There's nothing out here but more desert."

"I saw lights in this direction every night for several weeks."

"Now I see why you dragged me out here."

After another hour, Manuel loses patience. "Miguel, we need to head back, it is going to get late."

"Just over this hill, Dad. Please."

"Alright and then that is it."

They climb the slight incline as Manuel takes a drink. Miguel stops suddenly.

"What is wrong?" Manuel asks Miguel staring into the distance. A large white one-story building is sitting in the middle of the arid desert and is surrounded by a large chain link fence.

"Where are you going?" Manuel asks as Miguel walks towards the building.

"I want to read the sign on the fence."

"That is someone's property and looks important. Let us go back home."

"Just a little closer to read the sign and then back home, I promise."

Manuel smirks as he nods and they make their way down the hill. The facility looks almost abandoned except for black jeeps parked inside the fence and a helicopter port that is empty. They

can now read the sign: "Petro-Chemical Research Facility. No Trespassing Under Penalty of Law."

Manuel grabs his son's shoulder. "Come on," he says. Miguel turns but looks back at the sign. No words are exchanged as they head home.

As they arrive back at the village, Sarah and Laura greet them with food as they sit down on some old chairs in the main area near the well. Some villagers come out as the evening dies down and gets cooler.

"You boys have an adventure?" Sarah asks.

"We went out to the middle of nowhere," Manuel replies.

"We did find an oil company, though," Miguel added.

One of the eldest villagers, Hector Lopez, asks, "An oil company?"

"Not an oil company," Manuel says. "Or… maybe. I don't know. Had a sign on the fence that said Petro on it."

"It had an airport for a helicopter and cars inside of it but no one around," Miguel explains.

Raul Torres, called 'Donkey' the self-subscribed village idiot asks, "How did you know it was an airport for a helicopter?"

The Typical Day

"It had a big H on it, what else could it be? It also said no trespassing," Manuel says.

"Sounds like you two need to stay away from it," Sarah says.

"I agree, we should not be near it," Hector concurs.

"Maybe I should go and take a look," Donkey offers.

"You are not doing anything of the kind," Hector tells him.

Donkey looks down and walks off in a sulk.

Miguel looks over at Laura sticking her tongue out at him but quickly looks away when he catches her eye. Miguel shakes his head and looks back at the villagers. "That must have been the cause of the lights I saw in that direction the other night."

"Lights?" asks one villager.

"Yes, I have noticed lights out in that direction for long times most nights," Miguel explains.

Sarah looks down at Laura sticking her tongue out at Miguel and taps her on the shoulder. She looks up and says, "Well, that must be what it is."

"I don't know. It will just have to remain a mystery," Manuel says with a smile. "Good evening all. Thanks for the food, Sarah."

"You are welcome, Mr. Ortiz."

As everyone disbands, Miguel looks over at Laura staring at him. He sticks his tongue out and she looks shocked.

Sarah seeing this, smiles. "Come on, little lady."

Miguel catches up with his dad as they make it indoors. Miguel sits at the table and thinks quietly while Manuel sits down and works on his goat invention. As he polishes part of it he asks, "What is wrong, son?"

"Just thinking about that oil company out there."

"None of our business, Miguel."

"Yes, sir. Can I go stare at the stars? It is dark now."

"Not too late okay?"

"Yes, Dad." Miguel happily leaves to go to his favorite place on the rocks where he can see the village in the distance. The warm light of oil-based lamps glows and slowly turn out as the night progresses and it gets late. The light of the sun has long faded and stars now dominate the sky. Miguel stares at the constellation Southern Cross that shines in all its glory.

The Rival

Manuel is talking with several villagers about creating a new animal pen when Zane Flores walks up to inject himself into the meeting. Zane is the only son of Zora, widow, and woman of questionable character. Her apparent lack of morals has manifested in her son who feels he is better qualified to run everything in the village. As much as Manuel tries to keep him at bay he interferes. "What are we talking about?" says Zane.

Manuel replies, "Hi Zane, we are talking about building an extra animal pen."

"Why do we need that?"

"Well, some of the animals are developing issues with one another, being in the same area. Some are causing issues in the group."

"I haven't seen any issues. You sure about this?"

"Quite. Apparently, if you get certain leader types together, they clash. Best to keep them apart so they can do their own thing."

"Maybe you should just trust nature to pick a winner."

"It does not always pick the right one – just the meanest."

"I see. So, you think that the weak leader should still run his own pen despite his lack of ability to do it?"

"I am saying for the better of the majority of animals, the right leader needs to have a chance to keep a sane, peaceful herd."

"I don't agree."

"What about you guys, build the new pen or not?" Manuel asks the two other villagers, who nod, causing Zane to walk off in a huff.

"Why does he always have to be like that?" one villager asks Manuel.

"He needs his own pen," Manuel observes drily.

The men leave as Manuel goes to their collective stack of wood to work on a new pen. As he digs holes for the fence, he looks over at the traveling teacher who has arrived to teach the kids of the village. Miguel is very attentive and always trying to better himself with education. Manuel watches with pride. As much as he tries to keep Miguel with him, he knows his son is not meant for this life. It bothers him yet it gives a slight sense of hope for better things. Maybe Miguel can fulfill a life he could never have. Manuel looks over to Zane's home and Zane stands there with several people he hangs around with. A look of contempt is on his

face as he watches Manuel work. Deep in the pit of his stomach, Manuel knows he must deal with Zane. It is the nature of things.

Hector's Day

Hector Lopez is often called 'old man' out of respect since he is the wise one in the village. His walk is slow and his demeanor quiet. He observes the village and often serves as a mediator in disputes. He is the grandfather figure that takes care of everyone. A good-natured man that would give you anything he has. His responsibilities are light as his age restricts him from many hard tasks. However, he takes care of his pet goat.

Sometimes Hector's advice is not welcomed by the younger villagers as they feel they have a handle on things, but he is often vindicated when his advice turns out to be right. Still, he enjoys the respect of most everyone as they work and live as a family. He spends most of his time carving wood figurines from his chair, sitting in the shade and watching the others. He watches Zora being helped by her son Zane and Raul, known as Donkey. It humors him to watch Donkey's antics irritate Zane, driving him away, but it is just a tactic to be alone with Zora. Zora and Donkey act like they are just friends but everyone knows they are intimate.

Hector continues carving as he looks and sees Manuel, as usual, fixing things for someone. Miguel helps him but constantly wants to get back to his books on astronomy. Hector remembers a

time when he was young and wanted to be a rodeo professional. Opportunities are scarce in his part of the world and his dreams were never realized. He won one competition in his twenties of which he is proud. He sometimes relives those times in his head and enters the past where he rides again on his horse, Shadow who was black and fast. She knew tricks and could cut around barrels quickly. He became popular and was asked to join a traveling rodeo on tour. This was an opportunity he had dreamed of. He spent days learning the routines they wanted to demonstrate until one day a young girl came screaming her sister had fallen down a ravine and needed help. Hector jumped on Shadow picked up the little girl and rode fast out to the ravine. The girl was hurt but conscious and crying. He had no rope long enough to reach to climb down but saw a way around. Telling the young girl with to stay and watch for the others to catch up, he would ride around to get her sister. Negotiating a treacherous set of inclines Shadow stumbled, breaking her leg but saving Hector by bucking him off away from the ledge as she fell to her death.

"Shadow!" Hector screamed, but she lay lifeless at the bottom. However, he turned and picked up the injured girl and made his way back around up the hills. As he made it back to the

top of the plateau he was met by other rodeo people and locals. They took the girl from him and his rodeo friends asked where his horse was.

"She gave her life to save me and the girl," he explained and, with a tear in his eye, he left and just worked odd jobs till he settled in the village the rodeo had just visited. He has stayed here ever since.

Sarah walks up and asks, "Hector can you make me a bowl?"

"Absolutely, young lady. How big do you need it?" Hector asks.

Sarah motions at a size. "This big would be fine."

"No problem, my sweet."

Sarah looks down at what Hector is carving and she puts her hand on his cheek and smiles. As she walks away Hector looks down at the horse carving of Shadow and then looks back up at Sarah. "Shadow, my girl, you saved one fine lady," he says, putting down the carving and getting up to grab tools to start a bowl.

Zora's Day

From a young age, Zora Flores aspired to be a nun. She was a good kid and always respectful but her parents were con artists and spent their time in and out of jail. She would often help people but her parents' reputation meant people treated her with suspicion and she spent her time trying to convince people her intentions were honorable. Often, she would have to help people from behind the scenes without them knowing about it. She was fine with subterfuge if God knew what she had done.

When Zora turned sixteen she met a man in his early twenties who was suave and, in her eyes, perfect. Her ambition to be a nun faded when faced with this handsome man who called her Z. She could think of nothing else. Her parents did not care what she did as they were always concentrating on their next scheme. Zora's boyfriend, Javier, convinced her to run off and be with him. It was like a dream come true but after a few weeks, she came back to her parents upset and pregnant. The people were further convinced she was no good having a child out of wedlock and her boyfriend was convicted later of robbing a bank.

Her life shattered and having given birth to a child she named Zane, she moved far away. She moved into the village and drank.

No longer caring and self-centered she lived, hating life and never trusting people. Her son Zane inherited her emotions and grew up angry all the time. Every day she could see the face of her lover in her son reminding her of the failure of her life. However, she protected her son and gave into her vices. Donkey was a village fool but he was her fool as she saw it. It was her true weakness as she defended and took care of Donkey. Maybe it was the only person she felt she could help in the world. Even her intimacy was more to her a veil of protection to keep Donkey from needing anyone else and being taken advantage of. It was a strange twist of psychology but one that gratified her on some level.

Zora often eyed Manuel, finding him attractive. She makes a move on him sometimes but he always dismisses her as a drunk and easy woman. She knows his heart mourns for his lost wife Sofia and suspects his heart is being won by Sarah but she still likes to churn things. She also knows it infuriates her son, Zane, and maybe in a strange way it is how she gets back at Javier for his betrayal.

"Mom what are you doing?" Zane asks as he approaches Zora.

"What do you mean, what am I doing?"

"Drinking this early in the morning."

Zora's Day

"You should be more respectful of my drinking, Zane. It is partly your daddy too. Without it, you would not be here."

Zane walks away with a look of disgust. "Get out of my way, fool," he says to Donkey, pushing him aside.

Zora looks at Donkey. "Don't let him bother you, Raul," she says. "He is having a bad day." Zora laughs uncontrollably as she puts her arm around Donkey. "Come, boy, I have something to show you inside." They enter her hut for privacy.

Sarah's Day

Sarah has been a life-long resident of the village and owes her life to Hector and Shadow. Her older sister left in her twenties after finding love with a military man but later passed away in a house fire. Sarah has always felt indebted to her sister for saving her life by getting the help that fateful day. In a way, her sister had felt responsible for teasing her to walk so close to the edge of the ravine. It saddened Sarah that her sister was never close to her after that and lived with regret. Before she left they had a good day and cleansed the way between each other. Still, she misses her sister and her parents. Her parents were caring and gentle people that always worked hard and helped others. Her life was simple and early in her life she found a good man that gave her a child named Laura. He always looked to the future and left to find a life in America for them. However, he was killed working on a plantation in California and never made it back. She adjusted to focus on taking care of Laura and the strong foundation that her parents gave her made her strong and stable. Maybe this was part of why Zora felt jealousy towards her and constantly hit on Manuel. Zora knew Sarah like Manuel as she watched him constantly. Manuel reminded Sarah of her late husband and she felt a strong bond with

him. Manuel seemed to just relate to her only as needs happened never showing a visible interest in her. Yet she felt something deep inside they were meant to be together.

Sarah often undertook chores like cleaning clothes for Manuel and Miguel since Manuel helps her in many ways. She tries to interact but mostly her daughter Laura and Miguel seem to be the ones hanging out often. She stitches a hole in Laura's dress as Laura comes up to her.

"Mommy," Laura says.

"Yes, honey."

"Why does Miguel look at the stars so much?"

"Well, I think he sees things we are not aware of. Maybe he is figuring things out."

"I think it is just weird," Laura observes.

"Laura, that is not nice. Just because someone does something you don't understand does not make it weird."

"Yes, ma'am. Can I go hang out with Miguel?"

"Sure, sweetie."

Laura runs off as Sarah whispers to herself, "Weird."

Zane's Day

Zane watches as his mom and Donkey retreat into her hut. He continues digging a hole to make a new trough for his hogs. He does not like Donkey but he preoccupies his mom so he serves a purpose. As he digs he looks over at Manuel working. He does not know why but Manuel makes him angry. All he can do is stare with disrespect. Our great leader, I should beat him down just to show him how little he is. Look at his punk kid always staying up late staring at the sky. I hope something falls from it and hits him square in the head, he thinks.

He keeps digging as the hot sun just bears down on him. An old man with nothing better to do but carve wooden horses. Oh wait, looks like he will make something else now. Probably another bowl. People just like to keep him busy, is Zane's opinion of Hector.

Now that is one fine lady, he thinks as he spots Sarah in the distance. Too bad she wants that failure over there. He deserves no fine woman like that. She should come over to me and I will show her what a real man is. As he sees Laura running over to Sarah he thinks of how the village comprises bastard children. He chuckles as laughter turns to regret. He finishes digging his hole and pours

left-over food scraps into it saying proudly, "Here you go, pigs. Eat up and later I will eat you." He laughs as the hogs run over to the food. He just leans against his shovel and looks up at the sun. "It is hot," he says to himself. "Why in the world am I here?" He leaves and kicks out at one hog. "Out of my way, pig!"

Laura's Day

Laura has asked her mom if she could play with Miguel and having been given permission runs to find him. As she turns she sees Zane kicking one of his hogs and turns in disgust to look at her mother.

"Pay no attention to Zane, Laura, just go play."

"Poor piggy," Laura says, but the distraction of animal abuse is short-lived in the mind of this little girl. She soon moves to thinking about finding Miguel helping his dad last time she saw him. However, she is soon distracted by movement in the corner of her eye. Walking away from the village she looks around seeing nothing yet hears a rock moving to her side and turns. She walks toward with curiosity she cannot contain. As she comes around a large rock she confronts a large snake poised to strike. Frozen in fear she knows she is in terrible trouble and tries to slowly move backwards. Every time she shifts a little, however, the snake deepens its striking stance. Tears roll down her eyes as fear has gripped her solidly. The snake rattles furiously, focused on striking her when a large rock smashes it.

"He won't bother you now," Miguel says with satisfaction.

Laura runs and hugs Miguel. "I was so scared."

Miguel puts his arm around her and escorts her back to the village. “Come on,” he says soothingly.

As they approach the village the villagers can hear her crying and Miguel’s comforting words.

Sarah drops everything and runs to her. “Are you okay, sweetie?”

“I am fine, mom. It was a snake but Miguel killed it.”

By then Zane and Manuel have arrived while the other villagers seeing the gathering arrive.

“What happened, son?” Manuel asks Miguel as he approaches.

Sarah replies, “She was attacked by a snake.”

Sarah looks Laura over for bites. “I am okay, mom, he killed it with a rock,” she reassures her.

Manuel says, “Show me where it is, son.”

Miguel leads Zane and Manuel to the stone-crushed snake. Manuel moves the rock with a staff he has. The snake is lifeless and smashed as the dry earth drinks its life fluids.

“Good job, son,” Manuel says. Miguel smiles but does not feel proud, just glad it did not hurt Laura.

Zane picks the snake up. “Oh the pigs will like this,” he says and walks off with it.

Laura's Day

Manuel rubs Miguel's head and smiles as they start back. Zane passes the group which stares at him carrying the dead snake. Zora and Donkey emerge from the hut and Donkey run over to Zane. "Oh, I want that," Donkey says.

"This is for the pigs, fool."

Donkey runs over to the crowd as Zora just gives a "hmmm," and walks back into the hut. Donkey listens as Miguel regales the story to the villagers.

"Hey, you think there are more of them out there?" Donkey asks.

"They usually come in packs," Hector tells him. "Unusual for it to be coming here on the flats at this time of day. Something must have driven it out."

"I don't know," Manuel admits. "I and Miguel are going to look around for more."

"I am coming too," Donkey says.

"You be careful and don't play with them like the last time you saw one," Hector says.

"We will keep an eye on him," Manuel assures him. "Come on, Raul." The three hike around looking for companion snakes.

"Would you like some water?" Sarah asks her daughter.

"Yes, ma'am."

Sarah and Laura walk back to their home as Sarah says, "I bet you are dry after all those tears."

“Mom, Miguel protected me really good, didn’t he?”

“Yes he did, sweetie. Just like a big brother.”

Raul's Day

Manuel, Miguel, and Donkey are looking for more snakes as they circle the village outwards in a spiral. Donkey keeps picking up rocks and throwing them trying to hit bigger ones laying in front.

"You are pretty good at that, Mr. Torres," Miguel tells him.

"Donkey, call me Donkey."

"Son, address him by his proper name," Manuel says.

Miguel looks up at his dad. "Yes, sir."

Donkey looks around and throws another rock. Then states to Miguel, "If there is another snake, you know I will knock it dead with one shot."

"I bet you could, Mr. Torres."

"Hey, Manuel, why do you think that snake came all the way out to us? I thought they would stay nearer to the creek near the forest edge. This is pretty far away."

"You are right, Raul, but these rattlesnakes love the desert. Usually, they want more hill type terrain they can hide in. I am thinking something nearby must have driven some out towards us," Manuel replies.

"Maybe it was that building we saw," Miguel says.

“Yea I heard you guys talking about that. What about that building? Can we go there?” Raul asks.

“It is pretty far away. I think we should stay clear of it,” Miguel says.

“Come on, let’s take a look. At least tell me where it is,” Raul insists.

“You really should stay away from it. It looks serious.”

Raul looks disappointed and throws another rock. “You all think I am a big idiot and can’t take care of myself.”

“That is not true, we just worry about you,” Miguel assures him.

“You know I wasn’t always stupid. I was smart at one time.”

“You are still smart, you just have your own ways. Don’t let anyone ever tell you otherwise,” Miguel says.

They continue walking as Manuel and Miguel talk about father and son things. Raul’s mind drifts back to his early memories of his parents. He was six years old. His parents lived in the village and were told by a traveling teacher that Raul excels in spatial reasoning and seems to already grasp mathematics. The teacher tells them he is a prodigy, a rare child gifted and he must be cultivated in a special school. Having a hard time understanding

what the teacher is trying to explain and even more a mystery how their son got his brains from them, they agree to go with the teacher into the city and have their son tested for his potential.

The teacher brings them to the city to a psychological testing facility run by a local university where the professor and grad students give Raul a battery of tests. After hours of testing the professor brings Raul back to his parents and tells them he is very gifted and they have a program for children like him that is funded. He would be boarded and given an education commensurate with his gifts. They are proud and happy his future is bright and will become someone big. The professor tells the teacher to drive them back home while he makes all the arrangements.

On the journey home everyone is happy that Raul's talents will be put to good use when, suddenly, a large truck slams into the side of their car dragging it down the street. It turned out the driver had fallen asleep and ran the intersection out of turn. Police and medics arrive only to find one survivor in the car, Raul, who is in a coma and his injuries severe. The police brought several villagers to the hospital where the doctors explain that Raul has suffered much brain trauma. The villagers tell the authorities they will come back and take him home if he recovers.

After several months in a coma young Raul wakes up but he seems distant. He has a hard time talking and comprehending simple things even for a six-year-old. His injuries heal and the

villagers come back to stay till his release. He can walk fine and keeps looking around like he is seeing the world almost for the first time. The doctors tell the villagers he will need a lot of care as he has a hard time understanding but they say they will take care of him.

As they leave a nurse gives a toy donkey to Raul. Raul looks at it confused and the nurse says; "It is a donkey." She braes like a mule and Raul laughs. The doctor says to the villagers, "He will never be normal but he should be fine."

Only fragments of the accident reside in Raul's memory now but maybe that is God's way of keeping him happy in his condition. His mind drifts to a funny thought as he walks with Manuel and Miguel and starts to brae like a mule. Miguel looks up at his dad and Manuel gives a pitying look back. Raul laughs at the two as they return to the village.

The Man From The City

"Miguel wake up!" his dad exclaims as much of the morning has passed. "You have overslept again."

"Sorry, Dad."

"Well, get up because your uncle is here. He is unloading his vehicle."

Miguel excitedly jumps up and puts his day clothes on. Running outside he sees his dad and uncle by his uncle's jeep. "Uncle!"

Carlos turns around. "Migs!" They embrace warmly as Carlos bends over. "Guess what I have in this vehicle," he says.

"What?"

"Well, help me carry this stuff in and I will show you."

"Yes, sir."

They all carry in boxes of supplies into the house. Miguel is jumping with excitement, waiting to see what his uncle has brought from the city. Carlos opens a box marked 'Miguel's' on the side and pulls out some rolled up maps. His uncle rolls out the first one showing a map of the world. "You see, Migs, with this you can find the longitude and latitude of any place on earth."

"Wow, just like the one the traveling teacher had."

"That's right, but now you have your own." Carlos pulls out two maps of the night sky complete with star names and constellations. "Here is one for the northern hemisphere and the other for us in the southern hemisphere."

"Look, Uncle. There is the Southern Cross. I was looking at it last night."

"Very good, you remember the constellations well."

"Yes. I still have that astronomy book you gave me."

"What do you say, son?" his father prompts him.

"Thank you, Uncle."

Miguel hugs him as Carlos replies, "You are my nephew, it is no problem. Oh, but I have one last small item for you." Carlos pulls out a smaller box and sits down next to Miguel as Manuel walks over to look. Carlos hands over a leather case with a smile. Miguel looks at it carefully and opens the leather case to find binoculars.

"You know what that is?" his uncle asks.

"Yes, Uncle, it is bin-binoc-binoculars, right?"

"That is right, Migs. But these are not just any binoculars, these are military grade ones. Very expensive. They have the ability to see things far away in the day but at night can see better than your eyes. They are low-light binoculars."

"Brother, that is too much for him to have," Manuel tell him.

"Nonsense. He needs something to stare at the stars with and with these he can see them more clearly."

Miguel's eyes glow with pleasure. "Can I go outside and use them, Dad?" he asks.

Carlos looks up at his brother as Manuel replies, "Of course, son."

"Yea!" Miguel hugs his uncle and runs out the door. Carlos stands up and opens up one of the other boxes and laughs.

"That boy loves you but do you think it is good to give such gifts to him?" Manuel asks his brother.

"Why not?"

"Because the money for those binoculars could buy the village a manual pump for the well so we don't have to draw a bucket. Or, it could be used to buy Miguel new clothes. You know what I am saying."

"I know what you are saying. You want him to be just as miserable as you."

"What?"

"You heard me."

"Look, I love you and appreciate all this stuff you bring us but I afraid of the disappointment Miguel is going to have later."

“I think it is more the disappointment you will have later when that boy goes off to college.”

“College? He can barely write.”

“There is only one thing stopping that boy from his dreams and it is not his ability to write.”

“I raise my son the way I think he should be.”

“Yeah, because you were raised that way.”

“You forgot, you were raised that way too.”

“Yes, but I realized just because I was raised that way, did not mean I had to live that way forever.”

“Someone had to stay and keep these people living.”

“These people would live the same with or without you. You were just afraid of going out there in the world and becoming something different.”

“You think you are better than me, I know.”

“How many times have we had this conversation? I am not better than you, smell better maybe.” Manuel smiles.

“Now if you are done with this working man hero stuff let’s go to my jeep and get those pipes and pump out,” Carlos says.

“What! Pump, really?”

The Man From The City

"Yes, brother, this is my village too. You think I didn't hear the last dozen times you mentioned it. Had a time finding one I could transport easily."

"What about these boxes?"

"Ah, those are canned foodstuffs and tools for you to look at later."

Both men go out to the jeep and Carlos uncovers small sections of pipes enough to easily reach down the well with some to spare. Manuel gets his tools and Carlos unloads the material to run the pipes down the well. Some men come out to help.

Zane walks up. "A pump. Why do we need this?"

Carlos replies harshly, "Zane if you are not going to help, get out of here."

Zane walks off briskly, remembering his last altercation with Carlos and how he was beaten down.

Miguel is standing on his rock looking around all directions with his powerful new binoculars. He looks back at the village and sees the men and his uncle lowering his dad down the well, so runs back to watch what they are doing. Manuel sits on a swing board as he drives spikes into the the well wall that clamp the pipes steady. They lower him a little more till he puts enough clamps in all the way down. Then the men lower the assembled pipe down through the clamps down to the bottom where Manuel ensures the

pipe is far enough down in the water to draw from it. After he has tightened all clamps he is lifted from the well to draw a bucket of water.

"What are you doing, Dad?" Miguel asks.

"Well, we have to prime this pump by pouring water down the pipe to fill it up. That way the water will come up each time we pump the handle."

"How do you know how to do that?"

Carlos and Manuel look at each other smile.

"I had a job for a short time near town before you were born. I learned how to work on pumps," Manuel says.

Miguel looks at his dad with a new sense of amazement. Manuel fills the pipe up with water and the men attach the pump to the pipe and fix it solidly to the side of the well. By this time the whole village is watching.

"Take this pail and hang it on the pump nozzle," Manuel asks Miguel, who does as he is asked. "Now start pumping the handle."

Miguel pumps the handle repeatedly as the sound of something slurping keeps getting louder until, finally, water fills the bucket. The villagers yell in excitement as Manuel shakes his brother's hand. "Thanks, brother," he says.

The Man From The City

Carlos pulls Manuel over and hugs him. "We are all family here," he says.

Later that evening the village has turned out to eat some of the food and flavored drinks Carlos has brought and had a fiesta. Laughing and dancing go on as the music plays from Carlo's jeep. As the night goes on Miguel shows off his binoculars to the villagers and shows them the stars through it. They look in amazement especially at the moon that seems so close to them. Laura, however, prefers watching Miguel as he looks through them earnestly.

A song comes on the radio with no words. "Dad, what is that song?" Miguel asks.

Manuel and Carlos look at each other and the village grows quiet as many remember the song sung by Miguel's late mother. Manuel starts singing words to the music and the whole village is moved by the lyrics which talk about being amongst the stars. Miguel's heart moves in time with the song, a song not heard for many years.

"That is the song your mom sang to you long ago," Manuel explains. "We used to sing it together when I worked in town. I worked during the day and then we used to sing at a place people gather to have a good time called a club. We were good and made money. When you were born she used to sing it all the time to you.

When she became sick and passed away, I moved you back here. I went back to the life that made more sense to me."

Miguel is visibly upset and drops his binoculars to run off.

"Miguel!" his dad yells and turns to look at the villagers as Carlos picks up the binoculars and dusts them off.

"Come on, brother, let him sort it out."

The villagers disperse back to their homes cleaning up everything. Laura looks into the darkness in the direction Miguel went.

"Come on, Laura, he will be fine," her mother tells her and leads her away.

Miguel sits on his favorite rock crying. He looks up at the Southern Cross and asks, "God, why did you take my mom?"

The night breeze blows on him and as the time passes he feels calmer and at peace. He looks over at the village seeing the lights dim out as people are going to sleep. He feels little relieved even during his sadness he finally knows what the song was and the words to it. He looks up at the stars; "Mom I will find you among the stars like the song says. I promise." Miguel wipes his tears away and heads back to his home. He turns in quietly to bed as his dad and uncle turn in and let him sleep in peace.

Say Uncle

Manuel and Carlos get up and notice Miguel is already sitting at the table. “You alright, son?” says Manuel.

“I am okay, just thinking.”

“Nothing wrong with that,” Carlos says.

“Uncle, is that your company near us?” Miguel asks.

“What company?”

“There is an oil company to the west of us about seven kilometers,” Manuel explains.

“There shouldn’t be, this is not a drilling region.”

“No oil here?” Manuel says.

“No. This plateau is part of a government reserve, no drilling. That is why no one bothers villages like this. What did you see?” Carlos asks Miguel.

“A big white building with a metal fence around it. Had a helicopter airport and cars.”

Carlos looks up at Manuel. “It is true,” Manuel confirms.

“What do you say we take the jeep out there and take a look,” Carlos says.

“You two go, I have things to do. But be careful,” Manuel replies.

Miguel is excited. “Really?”

Manuel nods. "Really."

Miguel gets water bottles and his binoculars and his uncle drives them out to the facility.

"See, Uncle," Miguel says as they park on the hill in front of the building.

"Yes, I see. Let me have your binoculars."

Miguel hands the binoculars over as Carlos looks closely. He reads the orange sign but there seems to be no activity. A helicopter sits on the pad and several trucks and vehicles are parked around the building. He also sees a lot of crates.

"That is what you saw last time?" he asks as he hands the binoculars back to Miguel.

"No, there are a lot more vehicles. They only had a few cars here last time and those boxes were not there."

"Crates, shipping crates to be exact," Carlos tells him. "Does not make any sense why this is here. Let's head back. When I go back to the city tomorrow I will ask around about this."

As they drive back Miguel asks, "Uncle, how come Dad left working in the town?"

Carlos is quiet for a while before replying. "Our dad did not want us to go. Told your dad he was making a big mistake by

leaving. I had already left and he was wanting to make a life outside the village too. However, college was not for him, so he worked some skilled work, welding and working on machines. He was quite good and then he met your mom. They were very happy until she got sick shortly after you were born. The sickness kept growing and till it took her. Your dad took it very hard but not long after our dad died in an accident cutting a tree down. The villagers found him bled to death after accidentally hitting himself with an ax. Your dad felt like he had let everyone down and went back to the village to take care of everyone."

Miguel looks around. "Sounds like he wanted to go back to where things were simple and easier."

"You are a smart boy," Carlos says. "A simple life maybe, but not easy. Nothing easy about village life here. Our families have been here a very long time and the village used to have more people. A lot of people moved away for a better life." Carlos looks at Miguel and continues, "Don't ever look down on your dad for wanting to be out here."

"I won't, Uncle. I am proud of Dad. I never knew he could sing."

"He never sang before?" Carlos asks.

Miguel shook his head.

"He can sing like a bird and your mother an angel," Carlos tells him.

"I wish I got to spend more time with Mom."

"She is always around you, Miguel. She is with you, watching and protecting you."

Miguel smiles and they continue in silence.

"What do you think, brother?" Manuel asks as Carlos and Miguel arrive back at the village.

"That is no oil company. I am going to check it out when I get back."

"You leaving tomorrow?"

"Yea."

"Can I go play, Dad?"

"Yes, off you go," Manuel says. "You have a good ride with him?" he asks Carlos and Miguel disappears into the distance.

"He asked about you and your life before."

Manuel looks down at some tools he is holding and says nothing.

"When were you planning on telling him things? He is nearly a teenager," Carlos says.

"I don't know. I just find it hard to talk about."

Say Uncle

Carlos puts his hand on Manuel's shoulder. "No worries, let's get to work."

Later that night Manuel, Carlos and Miguel have a final meal together.

I wish you didn't have to go," Miguel tells his uncle.

"I will be back before you know it."

"Maybe next time Miguel can visit with you for a while," Manuel suggests.

Miguel's eyes light up. "Really, Uncle?"

"Why not? Let me take care of something and in a couple of weeks I will come back and pick you for a week with me."

"I am happy," Miguel says.

"That is good, son."

"Can I go look at the stars for a little bit before bedtime?"

"For a short time," Manuel tells him

"Yes, sir." Miguel grabs his binoculars as Carlos smiles and watches him leave.

"You just made that boy really happy, you know," Carlos says.

"It's not right to keep him locked up here all the time."

"Is this village a jail?"

Manuel looks at Carlos and smiles. "No. I just want him to be happy. Tell me something, brother. Do you really think he could be an astronomer?"

"I think he can be anything he wants. The only thing holding him back is latent guilt."

Manuel looks up sharply. "Yes, you might be right."

"We both know I am right."

The next morning Carlos is packed up and most villagers turn out to watch him leave. Manuel extends his hand to his brother and Carlos shakes hands with him but quickly pulls him into a hug and whispers in Manuel's ear, "Take care, brother."

They pull apart and Manuel smiles. "You too," he says.

Carlos kneels down in front of Miguel. "And you, young man, I will see you in two weeks." Carlos stands and rubs Miguel's head vigorously.

Goodbye, Uncle."

Carlos gets in the jeep and, throwing it in gear, says, "Keep looking up, nephew." He drives off waving at everyone as they all wave back. Miguel stands there as people move on to their daily tasks and he listens to the fading sound of his uncle's jeep.

Say Uncle

Manuel puts his arm around Miguel. “Son, go and play today. I got everything.”

“Okay, Dad.”

Manuel is cleaning his tools when hands rub his shoulders. It is Zora Flores also known as the ‘widow’. Ever since her husband died of a heart attack she has hit on every man in the village. “Hi, Man,” she softly says. Sarah is washing clothes in a wash bin watching them interact.

“What do you want, Zora?”

“Oh, nothing. Just wondered if there is something I can do for you.”

Manuel stops and stares at her for a moment and smiles. “I don’t think so,” he says, picking up his tools and walking away.

“You and I have a lot in common,” Zora calls after him.

Manuel stops as Zora walks in front of him and says, “We are both widows.”

“Not interested, told you before,” Manuel tells her.

“You say that but what could it hurt to have the love of a good woman?”

“Well, when one shows up let me know.”

Zora looks insulted and throws her hands to her hips. “Well, that is what I get for trying to be nice.” She stomps off back home as Sarah smiles and keeps washing clothes. Manuel looks up and

Zane is leaning against a post and spits at him as his mom walks by.

Hector walks to Manuel as he puts tools away. "Manuel, should we be concerned with that oil company?" he asks.

Manuel looks back to the west briefly. "I don't think so."

"I mean if they are an oil company, that drilling stuff can poison our well water."

"My brother is going to check it out."

"Okay, I hope we are not in trouble."

"I am sure the water will be fine."

"Yes, but if they find oil here, they will move us out."

"No one is moving us anywhere," Manuel tells him. "I will make sure that never happens. Besides my brother says this land is not capable of having oil drilled here because of government laws."

"Laws change with enough money. You think the government will care about a handful of villagers that don't even have electricity? I am telling you no one would care about us," Hector says.

"Someone would care. Look it will be alright old man," Manuel reassures him.

Hector walks away. "I hope so."

Manuel shakes his head and goes into his house.

Miguel is sitting out on his favorite rock showing Laura his binoculars. She pans around looking at everything.

"Don't look at the sun, it will really hurt your eyes," Miguel warns her.

"Silly. I am not dumb."

"What are you looking at?"

"My mom."

"What is she doing?" Miguel asks.

"She is walking toward your house but now is stopping."

"Why?"

"I have seen her do that once in a while. I think she likes your dad but is too afraid to talk to him."

"Why would she be afraid? She has known him for a long time."

"I asked her once but she told me to mind my own business," Laura replies. "You don't think they will get married someday, do you?"

"You as my sister, that is bad," Miguel tells her.

"Why is that bad? I would not mind having you as a brother."

"You are too weird?"

"*I* am weird? You are the one that sits up all night looking at stars."

"I want to be an astronomer."

"That is someone that looks at stars all night?" Laura asks.

"Yes."

"Weird."

"Not as weird as you being my sister."

"You know we could be married someday even if our parents married," Laura says.

"Now you are being really weird."

"It's true, we are not kin really. We would be brother and sister by marriage."

"I don't want to talk about it okay?" Miguel says.

Laura looks at the ground and kicks a rock. "Okay." She gets up and says, "I am going home now."

"Okay."

Laura looks back at Miguel staring through his binoculars. Miguel puts down his binoculars and watches her leave for home. He is not sure how to feel about Sarah being his new mom and puts it all out of his mind.

Carlos Apart

Carlos was never much for village life although he never forgot his roots. He is a city boy who enjoys large groups of people and the noise of an ever-changing landscape. He has had many loves in his life but never settled down. It is something that never suited him, nor have kids. However, he feels as if his nephew, Miguel, is like a son and enjoys spoiling him. It is his way of feeling what being a parent is like through his brother.

Carlos has no regrets, his life is full and happy despite having no attachments. Some people are built that way as he has told many ex-girlfriends, nearly all of whom felt they would be the one to turn him. However, he is a good man and most of the time remain friends with them. Some of his ex-girlfriends have even become friends with each other, like a club. The first of his girlfriends that married invited him to her wedding. He did not attend not knowing if it showed him up or out of genuine respect. However, he has accepted later invitations as he is happy for them. The grooms are respectful and happy to see him too as secretly they know that Carlos's steadfast attitude against marriage led them to find happiness. As he gets older permanence in a relationship pulls on him like the tide does from the moon. His

brother having Miguel has relieved some of that pressure for him that his family legacy would continue. Even better than Miguel seeks to be an astronomer and not a lifelong villager which gives him self-justification that his life has not been wasted.

One important woman in Carlos's past was named Eliza. She understood the rules of his life and she never wanted marriage either. A good friend and companion in life to talk to and help and be helped is all she wanted. She was a professional like him with her own career in graphic design. Though not married they were often thought of as a power couple. His relationship was always open allowing him and his girlfriend to date others, just to meet other interesting people. However, with Eliza, Carlos dated no one else even though she often did. She was beautiful, smart and always caring about his feelings. She even offered to not date anyone if that bothered him, but he would not restrict her. He often told her they were independent people with no strings attached. They never argued angrily and were always polite even when they disagreed. She would defer to his decision on important matters but he would never make that decision without respecting her

views. Friends would tell them they should get married, but they would just laugh it off.

Carlos brought Eliza to the village to meet his brother and Miguel when Miguel was eight years old. She took to Miguel like her own child and showed him how to make art. The two were inseparable. Other times she would help Sarah and the two acted like sisters. She may have been a city girl but had no problem with helping with the labor of village life. It made Carlos proud to see her dive in and not be ashamed of anything.

Carlos spent his time working as a design engineer for an oil-related company. It is good to work and pays well. His boss is very caring for his people and benefits are never scarce. This has kept his company very profitable having employees care for their own company. His boss's philosophy has been one of taking care of his people and they will take care of him. It is only good business and pays off eventually. Eliza came to work there and that is how they met. Working closely on many projects gave them the opportunity to know each other before developing the dating relationship they so richly enjoyed.

After several years of being with each other Carlos took Eliza out for a special birthday meal.

"Eliza, you are a true friend and I am glad to know you," Carlos says.

"You are a good friend too, Carlos. I hope our friendship will never end."

Carlos smiles and says, "I am sure it won't. I know we have not seen each other very much lately because we are so busy at times but I wanted to make up for that with a good birthday."

"Thank you, Carlos, you are always so considerate."

As they eat they are quiet and smile at each other sometimes.

"Carlos, I need to tell you something," Eliza says suddenly, breaking the silence.

Carlos responds with concern, "Of course."

"I met a guy a few months back and we have dated often. I think I am in love with him and he has asked to marry me. I know it is a short amount of time and seems stupid, but something feels right about it."

Carlos wipes his mouth with a napkin and takes a drink as they stare intently at each other. Finally, he says, "Well that is wonderful, Eliza. Are you really sure?"

"Well, he is a graphic designer like me and we share a lot of the same interests. Like you, he came from a small village, never been married. He has a fantastic sense of humor. I could go on and on but I won't."

"Hmmm, well it sounds like love. I am very happy for you both," Carlos says.

"I was hoping you would take it well and I asked him since he had no one friendly enough to him to matter if he would make you his best man. He said he would be happy to."

"I appreciate that but would it be okay if I passed on that? I feel uncomfortable being part of a ceremony, you understand?"

Eliza responds quickly. "Oh I completely understand and that is okay. You are just my best friend and I didn't want you to feel left out."

"You are my best friend too but I would feel better just sitting on the sidelines."

"Well I guess I should be going because my fiancé wants to do something for my birthday too," Eliza says after they have finished the meal in silence.

"Oh, I am sorry. If I had known earlier, I would have let you spend the whole evening with him."

"It is okay I was looking for a good time to break it to you," Eliza tells him with a smile.

"You are a smart girl to use your birthday in this way because you know I would not do anything to spoil your special day. You don't have to worry, I am happy for you both," he says.

"Are you sure you are okay?"

"Sure, why wouldn't I be?" Carlos says. "I have been dating women for a long time and never wanted any relationship to go further than friendship, you know that. We will always remain friends."

"Did he give you a ring?" Carlos asks suddenly.

Eliza excitedly says, "Oh yes." She digs in her purse pulling out a velvet blue pouch and pulls a diamond ring out of it and hands it to Carlos.

"Very nicely done on his part," Carlos admits and reaches for Eliza's hand. He places the ring on her finger and smiles at her. She blinks slowly and leans over to kiss him on the cheek saying, "Thank you, Carlos."

Carlos smiles and puts his hand on her cheek as she turns and leaves. He sits back down and takes a drink as she makes it to the door and turns to wave goodbye. He waves back and pays for the meal. He just stares at the chair she has just left and takes a few sips of wine. As he gets up he reaches into his pocket and pulls out a ring box and opens it to show a beautiful diamond ring. He closes the box and throws it on the table, grabs his coat on one finger lapped over his shoulder and leaves.

It Takes a Village To Make an Idiot

It Takes a Village To Make an Idiot

"Tell me about that oil company," Donkey says to Miguel as he returns to the village.

"What do you want to know Mr. Torres?"

"Call me Donkey. I like that better."

"My dad says I should address adults by a proper name."

"I am sure he did not mean me because I am not an adult really," Donkey says with a smile.

"You are old enough," Miguel assures him.

"Would an adult do this?" Donkey says as he gets on his hands and feet, kicks his back legs like a mule, and brays. "You see? Donkey?"

"Okay Donkey," Miguel agrees with a smile.

"Better. Now tell me about the oil company."

"Like I said earlier, it is just a big white building with a fence around it."

"Did it have guards like army guys?"

“No, it did not have anyone actually. I saw cars and a helicopter when my uncle and I went there. They had trucks this time too and big boxes. My uncle said they were shipping crates.”

“Bet you there is something valuable in those crates.”

“I would not go there and find out.”

“Right,” says Donkey thoughtfully. “You run along now. I got some things to do.”

Miguel walks away. “Donkey, please don’t go there,” he says when he sees Donkey deep in thought.

“No one is going there. I am thinking of something else,” Donkey replies.

“What is wrong?” Manuel asks Miguel later when he has returned home for supper.

“Donk… I mean Mr. Torres was asking me about that oil company.”

“Oh don’t worry about him, he is harmless.”

Miguel stops eating to ask, “What would they do to someone that broke in that place?”

“I am sure they would take them to jail,” Manuel tells him.

It Takes a Village To Make an Idiot

They both sit and eat not saying another word and the evening draws to a close.

"Dad?" Miguel asks

"Yes, son."

"Do you like Ms. Martinez?"

"Why do you ask?" Manuel asks after some thought.

"Laura says she sometimes seems to want to talk to you."

Manuel looks concerned and sits up. "Talk to me about what?"

"I don't know. Laura thinks she likes you. Do you think she wants to marry you?"

"Miguel, that is adult business. Besides she has a daughter and is a widow. She has a responsibility to take care of her young one."

"Just like you have a responsibility to take care of me."

"That's right."

"Wouldn't both of your responsibilities be easier if you married each other?"

Manuel is taken back by the insight. "I don't think we should talk about this," he tells Miguel.

"Yes, sir."

"Go to bed and get some sleep."

"Yes, sir."

Miguel sits quietly staring at the star appearing through the hole in his ceiling while Manuel puts his hands behind his head

and thinks about Sarah and what his son has told him. They drift off to sleep thinking of the same things.

The next morning Manuel is going to the well and pumping a pail of fresh water to take back to his house when Hector walks up to him with several other villagers. "Manuel, have you seen Raul?" Hector asks.

"Donkey?"

"Yes, no one has seen him."

"What do you mean no one has seen him? He's probably wandered off again."

"I don't think so," Hector says. He never usually misses his breakfast but he never showed up this morning. Some of his stuff is gone too."

"Miguel said he was asking about that oil company yesterday. Maybe he went to go look," Manuel says.

"Someone better go and see if he did. That fool could get himself in a lot of trouble," Hector suggests.

"I will go after there and see if he is there," Manuel says and carries his pale of water back to the house. He fills up water jugs and takes bread.

It Takes a Village To Make an Idiot

"Where are you going, Dad?" Miguel asks.

"Out looking for Donkey, he is missing."

"You think he went to the oil company?"

"It's a possibility. You stay here. Take care of the chores while I am gone."

"Yes, sir."

Manuel leaves heading west while Miguel goes to his rock and watches with his binoculars till his dad leaves his sight. He then returns to take care of chores.

After a long walk, Manuel makes it to the hill and slowly walks up to look at the facility. Again, there is no activity yet there a lot of crates and trucks there. Manuel walks around the facility but sees no sign of Donkey. He musters his bravery and yells; "Hello! Anyone in there?" No one replies.

"I am looking for a friend of mine, can you help me?" he shouts but receives no reply. Manuel heads south back towards the village to look for Donkey elsewhere but, looking back at the facility, he has an uneasy feeling that someone is watching him.

It is night-time and Miguel is worried while standing on his rock with his binoculars. Hector, Sarah, Laura and some villagers stand with him.

"You see anything boy?" Hector asks Miguel.

"Nothing."

"How can you see anything in the pitch dark?" Sarah asks.

"These binoculars can see things even in the dark," Miguel explains.

A short while later, Miguel makes out a shadow of a figure walking towards the village. "I see someone coming from the west," he says and everyone walks in that direction. Eventually, they rendezvous with Manuel.

"Dad!" Miguel exclaims.

"Son, everyone," Manuel says by way of greeting.

"Thank God you are okay," Sarah says.

"I am fine, just tired."

"Raul?" Hector asks.

"Never saw any sign of him. I take it he did not come back."

"No."

"I went to the oil company and yelled for help but no one was there. But they sure had a lot of stuff there. Much more than the first time I saw the place."

"Where do you think Raul went?" Hector says.

It Takes a Village To Make an Idiot

"I made a big circle around the village and back to the west side but I didn't see any sign of him. Tomorrow we need to form groups and go in all directions further out."

"Yes, first light," Hector says in agreement.

"I am glad you made it back at least," Sarah says shyly as the villagers disperse.

"It is good to see you too," Manuel says with a smile.

The whole village is up bright and early packing food and plenty of water. Manuel calls the villagers together.

"Okay people. We need to team up in groups of four and pick a direction. Miguel, Sarah, Laura and I will go west towards the oil company. You guys pick your directions and sweep back and forth to cover ground. Wider sweeps as you go out to cover more area. When it gets late noon then head back home."

Everyone acknowledges the plan and moves out. Hector and the older people stay behind for their own safety and if Donkey shows up. Each group sweeps pacing endlessly back and forth. Manuel's group makes it to the oil company and again it looks abandoned of people but even more supplies and equipment is there. There are also tanks sitting stacks with boards between each level.

"Are those bombs, Dad?" Miguel asks.

"No, son, those are irrigation or fumigation tanks. Like what crop dusters use to kill insects on large crops."

"What does that have to do with oil?"

"Not sure, son, let's keep moving."

They keep walking and leave the facility behind them. They make it almost to the edge of an oasis type area where the desert ends and pine trees create the beginnings of a forest.

"You think he made it this far?" Sarah asks.

"I don't think so," Manuel admits. "Just beyond that forest is the city. But the forest is pretty far and it would be foolish for us to try to navigate through it. Besides it is getting time to turn back anyway."

Having made wide sweeps they head in a straight line back to the village, eventually reaching the oil company again. They notice that things have moved around.

"Someone is here, Dad," Miguel says.

"Let's keep moving," Manuel tells them

They keep walking as Miguel looks back at the facility.

Eventually, when all the search parties have returned, everyone acknowledges that no one has seen Donkey.

It Takes a Village To Make an Idiot

"What do we do now?" Hector asks.

"There is nothing we can do. Either Donkey has left us for good or is dead somewhere," Manuel says.

"Well I think that is terrible to think he is dead," says Zora.

"He is just saying what we all are already thinking. We might have to accept the fact that Raul is gone," Hector tells her.

Zora paces off upset.

"Look we are all exhausted," Manuel says. "Let's just get some sleep before we say things we will regret."

"Sound wisdom." Hector agrees.

Everyone leaves as Manuel says to Sarah, "Thanks for helping us."

"Anything for you," she says with a smile and leaves with Laura who, as usual, sticks her tongue out at Miguel.

Manuel laughs. "Come on, son," he says putting a friendly arm around Miguel's shoulders.

Days pass and there is no sign of Donkey. Hector talks to Manuel. "I think it is a fact that Raul is dead."

"I think you are right," Manuel says in agreement. "We should talk to Zora since they were intimate."

"Yes, if you would do that I will talk to everyone else. We should have a memorial service for him."

"Agreed," says Manuel.

Manuel goes to Zora who ignores his presence.

"Zora."

She quickly replies, "I know why you are here, he is not dead."

Manuel looks to the ground and pans around. "He could not have lasted this long by himself with no supplies. He is gone, Zora."

Tears roll down Zora's cheeks as Manuel lifts up her chin and says, "You know this."

"He was stupid but he was nice to me," Zora sobs into Manuel's shoulder.

Manuel breaks the hug and says, "In that respect, he was better than us. We want to hold a memorial for him."

"Thank you," Zora says.

Zora walks into her home as Manuel leaves and sees Zane looking at him. Manuel nods and walks away as Zane looks to the ground.

The villagers hold a memorial service for Donkey that evening. They stand around the well and talk about the funny things he did and convey their feelings. Most are silent but some

cry, especially Zora close to him. Zane stands off from the crowd watching. However, everyone tries to put the obvious controversy out of their minds. As the days pass the village falls into a routine and for Miguel, the grief of losing Donkey has been replaced by anxiousness that his uncle will be returning in nearly a week.

The Dark Before the Dawn

The Dark Before the Dawn

Miguel has been looking at his star maps after dinner and asks his dad if he can go star gazing.

"I guess you have earned it, son. Try not to be out all night, okay?" Manuel says.

"Yes, Dad." Miguel grabs his binoculars to sit on his rock and watch the daylight give up its power to the cloak of night. The stars are bright and he stares through his binoculars at the gleaming lights that pierce endless space to reach Earth. He thinks about the time it has taken the light from stars to reach here and what he is watching is the past. Maybe even thousands of years' worth of light from distant stars. That star could be dead by now, but its light will shine as if it is still around, he thinks.

As he stares in amazement at the wonder of creation, he looks over westwards and sees a moving light in the sky. It is moving but not left or right and he wonders if it is a plane or shooting star. It is just above the horizon and only wavers back and forth slightly. Suddenly the lights go off and all he feels is a breeze and coolness of a draft as a wind blows past. He looks through his binoculars but sees no storms and the sky is still clear and full of stars. However, they look blurry so he adjusts his binoculars but nothing helps. He

feels very tired, too tired and sleepy to go back home so he lays down on his rock for a nap.

The following morning Miguel awakes in his bed.

Wake up, sleepy head," his dad tells him.

"What happened?"

"You fell asleep on your rock and I carried you back home."

"Sorry, Dad."

"Well, it was my fault for letting you stay out so late."

Miguel gets up and notices the table does not have his maps. "Dad, where are my maps."

Manuel looks around. "I don't know, they were on the table."

Miguel looks everywhere. "They are not here. Here are my binoculars but my maps are gone."

"They will turn up. Come down and eat," Manuel tells him.

Miguel sits down and has breakfast while his dad goes out to take care of the animals. As he arrives near the barn Hector walks up. "I have not felt better in my life."

"You too? I had a really good sleep."

"I feel really rested," Hector says.

The Dark Before the Dawn

Sarah and Laura walk up to milk the cows as Manuel asks, "Did you sleep well?"

"You know I really did," Sarah says.

"Seems a little cooler today too. You know it must be the seasonal change," Manuel observes.

"Might be."

Everyone attends to their chores. As Manuel finishes his, his attention is drawn to the fence he fixed weeks prior.

"What is wrong, Dad?" Miguel asks, walking up to him.

"Not sure, something seems out of place. I don't know. I feel too good to worry about it. Did you find your maps?"

Miguel looks disappointed. "No," he admits.

"Well, we will look for them right now, okay?"

They tear up their house looking for them but they are nowhere to be found, so they wander outside to see if the wind as taken them.

"I am sorry, son," Manuel says when nothing is found and, seeing Miguel is upset, he suggests he find Laura and play.

"I just want to go home, I don't feel like playing," Miguel tells him.

"Okay. I got to talk to some people, be home in a bit."

Manuel visits with other villagers and they tell him they feel good too but notice odd things out of place, although they can

express nothing specific. Manuel gets his pail and draws fresh water from the pump to take home.

"Hmm, that is strange," Manuel comments.

"What is strange?" asks Miguel.

"Come taste this water."

"It tastes different."

"I wonder if it has to do with that oil company like Hector said."

"What do you mean?" Miguel says.

"It is nothing to worry about," Manuel says with a smile. "You still upset about the maps?"

"Yes."

"You know what? Why don't you do some more stargazing tonight to cheer yourself up? But no sleeping out there again."

"Okay."

The night creeps in and Miguel goes to his favorite rock. He looks up at the night sky and notices something wrong. Panning back and forth across the night sky, he mutters, "It is not possible." Miguel rubs his eyes and looks around intently. Finally, a panic washes over him as he runs back home.

The Dark Before the Dawn

"Dad!"

"What's wrong, son?"

"Everything is wrong. Come outside."

Manuel follows his son to the well.

"Look at the stars, Dad," Miguel tells him.

Manuel looks up and says, "What I am I looking for?"

By this time some villagers have arrived to see what the commotion is about.

"The stars are all wrong," Miguel says to them all.

"What do you mean wrong?" Manuel asks.

"Look, they are out of place. Don't you see?"

"They look the same to me," Manuel says.

The villagers look around and mutter agreement.

"Look, you see that star, the faint blue one over there." Miguel points to it and his dad nods.

"That star is constant and tells us our longitude or where we are on the earth. It should be higher but is lower and in the wrong part of the sky."

Everyone seems baffled by his explanation, so Miguel explains further. "The Southern Cross is sitting in the west right now and it is just the beginning of the night. It should be in the East right now. Don't you get it?"

"Son you are not making any sense with that astronomy stuff," Manuel tells him.

"Miguel, what are you trying to tell us?" Hector asks.

Miguel looks at the sky once more. "We are not in Mexico anymore."

"What!? Of course, we are in Mexico," Manuel says.

The villagers laugh and Hector says, "Boy, you need some sleep."

"The stars don't lie. We are not in Mexico anymore," Miguel insists.

"Well, if we are not in Mexico, where are we?" Hector says.

Miguel grabs lamps from the people and places them on the ground to shine light the ground up. He grabs a nearby stick and draws the continents from memory. He points the stick at Mexico and says, "We were here but not anymore."

"Where are we then?" Hector repeats and everyone chuckles as Hector smiles at the group. Miguel ignores their humoring him as he takes a mental measurement based on everything he has learned so far. "Wait a minute," he says and runs to his house and finds his astronomy book.

"Manuel, is he okay?" Sarah asks.

"He is fine, just confused about something obvious."

Miguel runs back with his book and as he lays it down and on the ground to get the light. He opens to find certain pages talking about star locations and navigation by sailors. "If I had my maps I could find it easy but the best I can guess is we are here," Miguel says and points the stick to where he thinks they are.

"You are saying we are on an island," Hector says.

"Not an island, Australia," Miguel replies.

"What? Boy, you need a good night's sleep for sure."

"Son, he is right. You are not well," Manuel says.

"I am fine but I am telling you we are in Australia."

The villagers look up at the stars quietly for a few moments.

"Okay if we are in Australia then how come the village is here and the mountains are back there? Your rock is over there, our animals are here," Manuel asks him.

"I can't explain it. I just know it all looks the same in the day but the night is all wrong. You said that there was something not right about the sheep bin."

"That does not mean anything?"

"Why is it cooler tonight than last night?" Miguel says.

"The season is changing," Hector suggests.

"Come on, son, let's go to bed," Manuel says.

"Let me stay up and study the stars more."

“No. I think you need to rest. Sorry, everyone, we are going to bed.”

Meanwhile, in a laboratory in a white building marked by an orange warning sign, two men in lab coats are watching the villagers and listening to their every word. The scientists look back at their boss, the chief scientist and director Charles Tanner.

“Sir, should we abort and take them back to Mexico?” one scientist asks.

“Absolutely not, this Lazarus project must proceed. The Wright Foundation is funding us to succeed in this and it must move on. We knew there would be suspicions.”

“But, sir, the boy knows where they are.”

“He is a smart boy, but that is what these experiments are for. If we are going to successfully relocate villagers, tribesman and other peoples from areas needing resource extraction and development, we need to know we can fool them enough to reach acceptance of their new environment. And who forgot to leave the astronomy book behind?”

“We did not forget,” the scientists explain, “we just did not think it would help him. We left the maps his uncle gave him

behind because they had too much identifiable location information on them."

"Well, he figured it out anyway, the little punk. The euphoric drug seems to be keeping them not questioning the environment for now and they are not listening to the boy. Keep the same dosage in the well water and adjust the taste of the water to match the samples taken from the original well."

"Yes, sir."

Charles walks to the door and turns. "Gentlemen we have a mandate from Violet that this project must succeed no matter what. We need to prove we can relocate indigenous peoples from their home to a new environment without disruption to their lives or this is a failure. We have four weeks to prove this project a success before moving them back to their village in Mexico. Make this work guys.

The scientists nod as they change the water in the well to the natural taste.

Charles heads to his office and Jill Chambers his assistant director knocks on his door and enters.

"Sir, I understand we have a serious problem with the location awareness."

"We are proceeding, Jill, you knew this could happen."

"Yes, sir. That is an extraordinary young boy."

"And a good dynamic for our test," Charles says in agreement.

Jill walks to his door and asks, "Sir, do you ever question if what we are doing here is really necessary?"

"Never. Are you having issues?"

"No, sir. I just wonder if the thought passes my mind, it might other employees."

"It is your job to make sure any doubts or issues come to my attention."

"Yes, sir. By the way, the sedation treatment went well. Our subject is in a sleep state."

"Very good. Keep him on ice until further notice."

"Yes, sir."

Jill enters her office and stares at the monitors watching the village. She sees Miguel looking around and says to herself, "Come on, little man, put it together."

A New Dawn and a New Day

A New Dawn and a New Day

Manuel is up early feeling refreshed again and draws water from the well and as he pumps it he lowers his hand into the water to take a sip.

"The water tastes funny today?" Hector asks as he approaches.

"Tastes perfectly normal," Manuel says.

"Here, let me try," Hector says, taking a sip. "Much better," he agrees.

Manuel smiles and takes his bucket back to the house. "Hey, sleepy. Feel better?"

Miguel climbs down his ladder. "No."

"Have some water, it tastes normal. You will see."

Miguel takes a drink. "Okay that is back to normal," he concedes.

"Everything is normal. Tonight you will look at the sky and see for yourself."

"I hope so."

They feed animals and prepare for the day. Sarah walks up to Manuel. "I feel really good again today," she tells him with a bright smile.

"You know what? Me too. Say, would you like to have dinner tonight with me and Miguel. You know, you and Laura?"

Sarah grins shyly. "I would love to. I mean… I would like that very much."

"Well then, till tonight."

Zora witnesses the exchange with disdain and jealousy in her heart.

The scientist in the lab notices Zora jealousy and discontent.

"She should be even more euphoric from the drug in the water like the others," he mentions to his fellow scientist. They look puzzled but watch her on one of the mini cameras hidden everywhere. Then it occurs to them. "She is not drinking the water yet because she has been drinking the hidden booze she keeps there."

"Should we worry about it?" asks his colleague.

"No, just report it."

Back in the village, Manuel is working on laying feed down for the chickens. Zora approaches him. "I saw you with Sarah. Do you

pick that widow over another and for what? Because she is younger?"

Manuel looks puzzled; "I am not picking anyone."

"Sure. You let my little boy toy get killed somewhere. Maybe you even got him killed."

"What are you talking about?" Manuel asks.

"You got him excited about that oil company and your boy lured him over to it with smart talk. You knew he is not right in the head and you played him like a musical instrument. Just to get to me."

"Zora, you have been drinking. You need to go sleep it off."

"You know what I am going to do? I am going to go over to that oil company and burn it down. That's right. Maybe get a little revenge for Raul."

"You are not going anywhere but to bed.

"You want to take me to bed? Well, you are too late for that."

As Zora says walks away, Zane approaches and pushes Manuel away.

"You better leave my mom alone, understand?" he warns.

"What do you think I have been doing?" Manuel replies.

"I am just warning you."

Manuel walks away without a word.

Back in the lab, one scientist hearing this calls Charles Tanner. "Mr. Tanner, we have a problem."

The following morning everyone is about their business when one of the female villagers calls out for help. Manuel and everyone come running over to Zora's house where she is lying in bed with her eyes open. She is dead.

Hector confirms she has passed away. "My God," he exclaims looking at all the alcohol bottles laying around her. "Looks like she has died from alcohol poisoning."

Zane enters the house and cries out; "No! Mom!" Zane looks around at the villagers. "You all drove her to this. You never liked us," he rants. "You always wanted us to leave. And you…" he says looking at Manuel, "… you always think you know better than anyone how to run this village."

"We are all sorry, Zane, for your mom. Both of you are an important part of this village."

"That is crap, man!" Zane replies. "I should run this place, not you!"

A New Dawn and a New Day

Manuel steps backward as Zane walks towards him. "Look, Zane, this is not going to make things better," he says, holding his hands out in front of him.

"What are you afraid of? I think it is time to have a new leader."

"Zane, this is not the way to deal with your mom's loss."

"You are going to tell me how to feel about my own mom now, leader?" Zane takes his shirt off and keeps walking to open area of the village as Manuel walks backward. Miguel runs up and looks in shock as the rest of the villagers gather around.

"Zane let this go," Hector tells him.

"Leave me alone, old man. He is the one that took your job away from you."

"You are wrong, Zane. I asked him to run the village."

Zane looks over with hatred at Hector. "That figures. You are just as foolish as him."

"Knock it off, Zane," Manuel tells him.

Zane and Manuel keep slowly moving. Manuel looks over at Miguel and then looks back up at Zane and stops. Zane stops as well and looks puzzled.

"Alright, let's do this," Manuel says suddenly and charges.

The two collide falling to the ground, dirt enveloping them as the fight ensues. Both men trade short punches rolling around on

the ground and then break apart to stand. Zane throws a punch which lands on Manuel's face but Manuel comes back with another hit that knocks Zane backward. Zane rushes him and knocks them both almost over into the well. Manuel yells out from hitting the well but kicks Zane backward. He then jumps Zane and they roll, punching more till the two are worn out. They roll on their backs and lay next to each other kicking each other with what little energy they have left. Miguel stands close, looking at the two beaten and bloody men.

"Feel better?" Manuel asks.

Zane rolls his head over and the two men look at each other. Zane laughs and Manuel smiles.

"Maybe a little," Zane admits.

Manuel stands and holds his hand out to Zane as he grabs it and stands. "Sorry for your loss," he says.

Zane puts his hand on Manuel's shoulder and staggers off while Miguel grabs his dad and helps him sit near the well. He pumps water out on his dad's shirt and helps clean him up.

"That was some fight, Dad," Miguel says.

"It was what he needed."

"I don't understand."

A New Dawn and a New Day

Manuel explains. "He is hurting for his mom and hates everyone. In a strange way, I had to fight him to give him a chance to work it out."

"You men and your ways," Sarah says.

"It worked didn't?"

"Worked getting yourself hurt but, yes, I suppose it worked."

They continue to aid Manuel as the villagers disperse back to their homes and tasks.

That evening Zora is buried east of the village.

"Lord take her into your arms. She was a caring and giving person but when she lost her husband, the alcohol seemed to be her only friend. Raul came and kept her company and now they keep each other company in heaven. Bless them both and her son Zane. May they both rest in peace together Amen." Hector finishes the blessing and after a little silence, the villagers return home.

"She was an extraordinary woman," Manuel says.

Zane stands quietly as Manuel turns to leave. "Manuel," he says. Manuel turns to look at Zane. "Thanks," Zane says as he continues to look at his mom's grave. Manuel nods and walks away.

Behind the Curtain

At the research laboratory, Jill comes into the chief's office to discuss the issue weighing on her mind.

"Chuck, I am very concerned about the Zora incident," she says.

"You only call me Chuck when you're angry. What Zora incident?"

"The incident I am talking about is killing her. Did we really have to do that?"

"You're a clinical psychologist and read the risk assessment on her threat to come here looking for her lover."

"I know she threatened it but she was an alcoholic and frustrated. I don't think she would have made good on the threat. Even if she did, what could she do here but beat on a fence?"

"She would have had the whole village over here looking for her and furthered their need to figure out what this facility is. Besides her biological profile suggests she had a failing liver anyway," Charles says.

Jill disagrees. "I think they would have just left with her. Anyway, don't hide behind her liver."

"I am not hiding behind anything and I have to disagree with you there. It is my belief it brings unwarranted attention to this place when we need them to focus on their village life. So, she needed to die. Also, another disappearance like her lover would have given the villagers a serious alarm to do something. We needed her to no longer be a nuisance to the project."

"Nuisance? There was not supposed to be any human deaths in this project."

"You knew there could be when you signed the project contract. Look, you know how important this project is. If it had not been for the Lazarus Game halted long ago that would have given us much of the behavioral information to start and we could have done this on a voluntary basis. But we had to move to phase two of this human reallocation project in a more abrupt manner."

"I understand that," Jill says, "but I am not comfortable with bringing hard realities like death into the fantasy of the project."

"Look if we don't learn how to relocate primitive peoples onto a reservation enabling them to keep their normal quality of life, we will have a catastrophe like the Native Americans endured in the old west. Do you want that? Progress is going to happen, we can make it equitable for all."

"I get it. I just know there is always a way to rationalize any action with a seemingly good intention. But you are hiding, hiding in this building."

"Well you can leave anytime you want," Charlcs tells her.

Jill pauses knowing that if they are prepared to kill an innocent villager then nothing would stop them doing the same to a potential whistleblower. "No, I believe in the project," she states.

"Alright. What is the acceptance level of the drug?"

"They have not questioned their environment much. Despite the slight changes in the mountainous region, soil slight differences, it seems to have been overlooked. I think we can start scaling the drug down."

"Okay, but be cautious. As you know we do not want to lose the general consensus that they are moved. If they get to that point the experiment is tainted," Charles says.

"Yes. One thing that did happen is a goat was sick but we replaced it last night just in case the other one died. Also, the region has worked well and is devoid of indigenous bird species flying over this area. They tend to route around the mountain range out of site. However, there is a risk of some land life infecting the zone."

"You mean reptiles, mammals?" Charles asks.

"No. We screened the area out beforehand well and have sensors to watch intrusions. I am talking more about insect life.

They tend to not be swayed like animals and go where they want. It has not been much of a problem on crawling ones as the insecticide barrier has kept them out, but flying ones could pose a problem. There are some in this country that is especially drawn to the village and fires."

"How do we deal with that if it happens?"

"I have proactively introduced these insects and animals that could show up, into a school book for the tutor to make the kids aware of. They can tell them they are rare. That way if something is seen, the kids will say they saw it in the school books."

"Good. Anything else?"

Jill keeps her composure hoping the report has taken his mind off her concerns. "No, sir," she says and leaves his office with a smile. As she exits she goes to her office and backs against the door holding her chest trying to breathe steadily. She is panicked but is trapped. She goes to her desk and watches the monitors of the villagers and continues her assessment for the project.

Meanwhile, Charles makes a call. "May I speak to Ms. Wright?"

"What do you need, Mr. Tanner?" asks Ken, Ms. Wright's executive-in-charge.

"Hello, sir. I was just reporting to Ms. Wright that we may have a slight issue," Charles says.

"She is busy. What is it?"

"My assistant director, Jill Chambers, seems to be having second thoughts about the project. It has me a little concerned."

"Is it contained?" Ken asks.

"Yes, she is compliant but we had a forced death in the test group and it seemed to upset her."

"One moment." There is silence on the phone for a while and then Violet Wright who is in charge of the project and its financing comes on the line.

"Charles, let me make this perfectly clear. I want no unwarranted attention to this project in any way. I have a person on my end that is making a lot of trouble for me and this project must continue for my client's sake."

"I understand ma'am, that is why I am making you aware well ahead of time," Charles tells her.

"It is appreciated but I need to know the confidence level you have."

Charles feels a little worried knowing what these people are capable of. "I think she is stable and my confidence is good. If it becomes a tangible problem, I will inform you immediately of course," he says.

"Good. I hand-picked you for this because of your track record of getting things done. Don't let me down."

"Absolutely Ms. Wright." The phone hangs up on Charles abruptly as he slowly hangs the phone up and looks around the office. He sighs and runs his hands through his hair.

Jill approaches the control room and orders the drug dosage decreased by fifteen percent with close monitoring closely. She stares at the monitors of the village as a worker asks, "Anything else ma'am?"

"No, you guys are doing good," she says.

Back There

Back in Mexico, Miguel's uncle Carlos is talking with various people on the phone about the petrochemical company outside his old village, but no one, including the government, seems to know anything about it. Some even doubt there is such a facility there. Making no progress, Carlos decides he must go back and take pictures of the facility as proof. Making the long trek back to the village he sees the remnants of the village but most things are gone and no one is around. It looked like it had been abandoned for days.

"What the good Lord has happened here?" Carlos mutters to himself and goes into his brother's partially made home to find Miguel's maps sitting there. He gathers the remaining belongings left behind and puts them in his jeep. Carlos looks around in all directions feeling very concerned then looks toward the petro facility. Driving his jeep towards the facility he makes it over the top of the hill to find nothing there.

"This is the place, I'm sure of it. Where is it?" he says, now thoroughly baffled. He drives down and sees only flat dirt and rocks like everything that was there simply vanished. He walks around the area that recently contained a large building. He paces

around and kicks a rock which uncovers a metal part that looks like a strange bolt. Kneeling down he picks it up and stares at it. Standing he puts it in his pocket and heads back to the village. He stops and looks at the ghost town.

"As God is my witness I will find you, Miguel. All of you." He throws his jeep into gear and goes fast back to his hometown.

Carlos sits on his bed and stares at the bolt. First thing in the morning he gets up and calls the police and even the military but no one takes him seriously. He looks again at the bolt he found and goes into work to see if someone there knows what it could be and to ask his boss for some time to figure out the mystery of the disappearing village.

None of the engineers in Carlos' workplace know what the bolt is, but when he asks his boss he gets a suggestion.

"You know I could be wrong but this looks like a part of a military vehicle. The metal type and design are very precise, which usually means military. Where did you get it?" his boss asks.

"My old village is gone like they all just packed up and left. Since they have no phones, I have no idea where they went. But before they left they were all perplexed by a petrochemical facility

nearby. I went to it after discovering my village was gone, and the facility was gone too. I found this lying in the dirt."

"Maybe they got bought out to move elsewhere? Especially if a company found oil there."

"That is the only thing I can think of, too. However, why would my nephew leave his star maps there? I just feel something is terribly wrong," Carlos says.

"You need some time off to go investigate this," his boss suggests.

"Is that alright?"

"Carlos, you are a good employee and you won't be any use to me worrying about your family. Go and figure out where they moved to."

"Thank you, sir. I think I must first confirm exactly what this bolt is and if it is military."

"You know, I have a buddy that worked on all kinds of military machines. I bet he would know. I'll arrange for you to meet."

Later that day, Carlos hands the bolt to his boss's contact. "What do you think?" he asks.

The owner looks at it and pulls out precise measuring instruments to analyze its dimensions. "That is what I thought. I can confirm it is military," he tells Carlos.

"From a jeep or other military transport?"

"Not a jeep, a helicopter."

"Helicopter?"

"This is a replacement part for what is most likely handles the foot pedals for the rudder or what is sometimes called the anti-torque pedals. You see I know it is a replacement part because it is not stressed on the threads as if it was used yet. It is virgin in its composition. Someone simply was undertaking maintenance on a chopper and dropped this. Where did you find it?"

"There was a petrochemical facility near a village I grew up but they packed up and moved the entire place. This was the only thing I found in its original location," Carlos explains.

"I doubt that was a petrochemical company," the owner says. "It had to be military."

"Military, how?" Carlos asks.

"I am not sure because it does not make sense that you found it around here."

"Well, I saw the facility and it had a helicopter pad there."

"That is not what I am driving at. The part does come from a military helicopter but not from one of our own."

"What?"

"The measurements are wrong and the style also, for what we use even today."

"If that is not ours then who does it belong to?"

The owner stares at it with a magnifying glass to double-check. "American," he asserts.

"American? You sure?" Carlos says.

"Yes, definitely."

"So I found a part of a helicopter that was obviously there because they were fixing it, in our country where there used to be a fenced-in facility claiming to be an oil company."

"Look, I do not know what you are mixed up in but if I were you, I would just throw this part back out there where you found it and forget about it," the owner tells Carlos.

"I can't."

"Well, it is not my business and I really don't want to become further involved. Good luck to you, sir."

Carlos stands up and shakes the owner's hand.

As Carlos makes it back home he calls a local military base and asks if he can meet with someone in the army. He says that he found a piece of military parts and would like to return them. The officer on duty puts him on hold and then grants him a visit for tomorrow. The next day he heads to the base and after being

cleared through the gates he meets with Colonel Garza, the regional security chief. "Hello, sir, what can I do for you?" he says.

"I hate to take up your time, sir, but I grew up in a village called Las Oilas on the east outskirts of Michoacán."

"Oh yes, I have flown over that area before," Colonel Garza says.

"Recently?"

"No, not for a long time. The region is very limited in population or military significance."

"Well, I think it has significance now." He hands the bolt over to the colonel.

"What is this?" Colonel Garza asks.

"I had a friend that used to work on all things military and he tells me that is a rotor bolt from a military helicopter."

"Yes, but why is it important?"

"It belongs to an American helicopter and I found it next to my old village."

Colonel Garza laughs. "I seriously doubt that, sir. We would know if American helicopters were flying in our country."

"Apparently you don't because this one did not fall off a helicopter, it was used to repair one on the ground, and I know where that repair happened."

"Over at Las Oilas?"

"Not exactly. West of it just a few kilometers away. But this is a clue to something much more important."

"What is that?" the colonel says.

"My old village is gone – most of the structures and the people."

"Okay, this conspiracy all sounds a bit far-fetched."

"Come with me to see," Carlos insists. "The village is almost entirely gone. My brother and nephew are gone."

Garza sees the controlled panic in Carlos. "Tell you what," he says. "I will look into it."

"Not good enough. This bolt is proof that someone has been here that should not be, agreed?"

"If, in fact, this is a part of an American helicopter then yes, it does raise concerns but it also asks the question of how you came into possession of it."

"Please come out and look at the village with me. I will show you where the facility was that used to be there. That is where I found that bolt."

"What facility?"

Carlos explains. “I saw it the last time I was visiting with my nephew and brother. It was white office buildings with a helicopter pad and fence. It had containers as if they were preparing for something.”

“Were there Americans there?” Colonel Gaza asks.

“I did not see anyone. I got the feeling they were there and knew we were watching them.”

“I see. I am going to ask you to make a complete statement to one of my men and then we will study it.”

“It may be too late by then.”

“Too late for your people?” Colonel Garza says. “What do you think happened to them?”

“I know you don’t believe me but whatever happened to that facility is what happened to them. The place shows up and as far as I can tell, no petrochemical facility has any business there.”

“It is a petrochemical facility now, not a military base?” Colonel Garza asks, confused.

“Please take me seriously. The sign on the outside said it was a petrochemical facility but I know from my job in the oil business, there is no need for a facility of that kind out there. The bolt proves

it was a military installation and obviously covert since you act like you don't know anything about it."

"Alright. Sir. The only thing I can do is make a report and I will look into it."

"Okay, but please do something about it."

"I take my job seriously. If I say I will look into it, I will."

"Thank you," says Carlos then escorted to an administration office where he fills out a report on what he saw. Afterwards is escorted off the base and returns home, worried about his family and the other villagers.

Desperate and concerned he contacts people related to the villagers that live in other towns and cities but no one has heard from any of them. The school tutor reports she saw military type vehicles leaving the area recently but just assumed they were moving on.

Carlo sees no option but to call someone he never thought he would talk to again – Eliza Gomez, his old girlfriend.

"Hello," a familiar voice says on the end of the line.

Carlos hesitates for a bit then says, "Eliza, it is Carlos."

"Carlos, oh my goodness. How are you?"

"I am fine and you?"

"Fine. Surprised to hear from you, though."

"I know it has been a long time but I need your help on something."

“Of course, anything.”

“You remember visiting my old village?”

“Yes.”

“Well it is gone and I do not know where they all went to.”

“Gone? Did you say gone?”

“Yes, the villagers and most of the buildings. All their possessions are gone except for some maps and things I gave Miguel.”

“Did they move somewhere?”

“That is what everyone thinks.”

“But you don’t believe that?”

“I think something happened to them, especially with that facility gone.”

“What facility?” replies Eliza.

Carlos explains to Eliza, all his findings over the past couple of days, up to the point of being told his discovery of a strange bolt was American in origin.

“American?” Eliza exclaims.

“Yes. An engineer with experience in military hardware says the design is definitely American.”

“What would Americans be doing there?”

"Not sure, but it seems they were posing as a petro company."

"They would have to be working with our government, surely?"

"Maybe, but for some reason, I do not think so. Anyway, I was hoping for some distant reason one of the villagers might have reached out to you. No one seems to know anything and the tutor that goes out there to teach school saw they were gone and even saw military vehicles leaving."

"Were they American?"

"She did not say, just military looking."

"It has to be a joint military venture that is secret and they might have moved the villagers for their own safety," Eliza suggests.

"Maybe, but I really think something is badly wrong here. I am going out tomorrow to look around again."

"Let me go with you.

"Thanks, but I don't want to take you away from your new job at your husband's company."

"I can take time off."

"Are you sure?"

Eliza laughs. "I am sure. Let me help you."

Carlos responds with a sense of relief that someone is on his side. "Thank you, Eliza, you are the best."

"Anything for you, Carlos."

The following morning Carlos waiting for Eliza to show up as he packs water and a metal detector. The doorbell rings and Carlos takes a deep breath.

"Eliza you look as lovely as ever," he tells her.

She smiles as they hug. "You look great yourself, Carlos."

"Come in. I'm just finishing up packing some things."

"Place looks the same," Eliza observes, looking around.

"Yea, you know me. I don't change much."

She notices he still has a picture of them together and picks it up. Carlos notices and says, "Remember that day when we were visiting the village and Miguel took our photo?"

She runs her hand over the front of the photo. "How could I forget?" She puts the photo back and turns with a smile. "So, what are we bringing?"

"Oh, just some beverages… and I bought a metal detector."

"You want to find some more evidence, I take it?"

"That is right."

As Carlos drives out of the city on the long distance road through the desert they are quiet. She looks at him sometimes and he would sometimes glance back and smile. She finally breaks the

silence and says, "I had forgotten how far the village is and how arid the land is."

"Oh yes, but time seems to pass quickly though," Carlos says. "By the way, thank you for coming with me."

"No problem," Eliza replies with a smile.

Carlos finally builds his courage to ask, "Your husband is not going to have a problem with you going out alone with me is he?"

Eliza stares down at her feet. "Actually we are not married," she admits.

Carlos looks at her puzzled.

"We went through the ceremony and all, but the night of our honeymoon I told him I did not feel right. We eventually had our marriage annulled."

"Wow. What happened?" Carlos asks.

"I don't know. He was a good man and we were very compatible. I am sure I would have been happy spending my life with him but it just did not feel right. I mean I still work with him at the company and we get along. I think he understands and he is dating someone new now."

"I am sorry it did not work out. You could have talked to me about it if you needed to. You know I am there for you, my friend."

"Oh I know, but I just wanted to be alone for a while and sort it out," Eliza says.

“I can understand that. It is weird we never hooked up and talked about it all this time.”

Eliza looks at him. “It is weird, isn’t it?”

They continue the drive quietly until they arrive at the village.

“Oh, my Lord, what has happened?” Eliza says, stepping out of the jeep.

“You feel it too?” Carlos asks.

Eliza walks around, “Yes. What happened to all of them? I mean why would they take part of their homes but not other parts. It makes no sense.”

Carlos sets up his metal detector and begins to scope the area for loose metal. Eliza looks at the well and says, “Why would that take all the stones from the well all the way to the bottom?”

Carlos walks over. “You are right, that is even more unusual.” Carlos continues to scan for objects with his detector as Eliza continues to investigate, walking to where Miguel and Manuel’s home is and shaking her head in confusion.

They head to the location of the facility and as Eliza steps out of the jeep she agrees there used to be something there.

“What makes you think so?” Carlos asks.

“This area is level and flat and a perfect square.”

Carlos smiles and replies, “Exactly.” He scans the area for metal with his detector.

Eliza walks around and finds a clump of dirt and picks it up. Her hand feels numb so she drops it. She rubs her numb hand with the other and the other hand tingles too.

Carlos sees her panicking and runs over. “Are you alright?”

“I picked up that clump of dirt and my hand started going numb and now rubbing it my other is feeling weird as well.”

Carlos pulls a water bottle out and pours it on her hands as she rubs them together. “Much better,” she says as the sensation leaves.

“Better now?”

“Yes, I am fine now. What is in that dirt I wonder?”

“I am getting a bag to put it in,” Carlos says. “It must be some kind of chemical residue left by the place that was here.”

He hands Eliza the bottle of water to finish washing her hands as he retrieves a plastic bag and rag. He reaches down and puts the clump of dirt in the bag being careful not to let it touch his skin, before taking it to the jeep and putting it in a container.

Eliza takes the remaining water and pours it over Carlos’s hands. He stares at her cleaning his hands and he realizes his feelings for her are as strong as ever.

Carlos smiles. “Thank you,” he says.

Carlos continues his scan of the area with a detector finding nothing as Eliza sits in the jeep drinking water.

“Nothing, absolutely nothing,” Carlos says as he throws the detector in the back of the jeep. “Well let’s get you back home.”

“Thank you for coming with me today,” Carlos says to Eliza as he walks her back to her car.

Eliza smiles. “Of course, Carlos. If you need me to help you, please just let me know.”

“I will keep in touch. I need to find out if the military has got any news.”

“You know the media might be able to help. Tomorrow, how about I call around and start trying to stir up interest and maybe if they cover the story, someone will see it and know what happened.”

“Brilliant, thank you!” Carlos says, as Eliza kisses him on the cheek and takes her leave with a smile and a wave.

The following day Eliza spends her time calling around to every news agency and anyone that might have a clue what has happened or at least shows an interest in the story. Although she garners only

mild interest, she continues to try. Meanwhile, Carlos calls the military base to talk to Colonel Garza but they tell him the colonel is away from base checking out a report. Carlos, realizing the colonel might be at the village rushes out to meet him. On his arrival, however, he finds the area cordoned off by the Mexican military.

"Sorry, sir, no one is allowed in this area," a soldier tells him.

"My family lives in that village and I am the one that told you they were missing," Carlos explains.

"What is your name, sir?"

"Carlos Ortiz."

The soldier picks up his radio and talks to his commander. "There is a Carlos Ortiz on the west perimeter that claims he is related to the villagers."

"Escort him to the village," the soldier is told.

"Yes, sir. Please get in your vehicle and follow us," the soldier tells Carlos.

On his arrival at the village, Carlos sees a team of army people taking pictures and examining the area.

Colonel Garza steps over to Carlos. "Mr. Ortiz, as you see I am looking into it."

"Thank you, sir, for checking it out. Have you found out anything?"

“We thought at first your relatives and the other villagers simply left and packed what they could, but there are anomalies. Like why would they leave only parts of homes and not the most important structural parts?”

“I was out here before and found my nephew’s maps,” Carlos tells him.

“Why leave maps and other things that might help them navigate around?”

“I gave those maps recently to my nephew, Miguel. My ex-girlfriend and I were out here yesterday and she found a clump of dirt at the location of the petro company I told you about. The dirt made her hand numb and we had to wash it off. I have it in a bag and was going to bring it to you when they told me at the base you were out. I figured you were here.” Carlos reaches into his container and pulls the bag out.

“Did you get medical treatment?” the colonel asks him.

“No, she was fine after we washed it off.”

“It sounds like a neuroinhibitor. When used as an aerosol, it creates sleeping gas.”

“You know about it already?” Carlos says.

"Yes, we found an area of ground where it might have spilled. That must be the clump your girlfriend picked up. We also found traces on the dirt around this village and nowhere else."

"Is it dangerous? Should my girlfriend, I mean ex-girlfriend, seek medical attention?"

"It is inert after it makes biological contact and dissipates over time. Which means when it was deployed, it happened recently, like within a week," the colonel tells him.

"Deployed how?" Carlos asks.

"Plane, or even a helicopter."

"Helicopter," Carlos says with a nod.

"What is also disturbing is we found a mass grave of animals nearby."

"What?"

"The grave contained a variety of goats and chickens that were apparently killed by a gas of some kind and then buried."

"How do you know it was gas?"

"Because to kill a variety of animals like this that do not cohabitate means you have to gas them to kill them all at once. Then you can scoop them up and bury them. I know what you are going to ask next, how do I know they were killed at once? The answer to that is in open air gas is not controllable where it goes so you have to aerosol it in a wide area to get everything which means they all died at once."

Carlos looks very concerned. “Does that mean the villagers, Miguel was –”

“No, they were not,” Colonel Garza interrupts.

“How do you know?”

“For one thing there is no mass grave for the people. Secondly, if you were going to kill them all and make an entire village disappear you would not leave traces of the village. No, these people were taken, not killed. Most likely put to sleep by that chemical you found.”

“Who could take them without you knowing it?” Carlos asks.

“Someone with the resource and ability to infiltrate our country and do it right under our noses. The bolt you gave me is an American helicopter, one of their military ones.”

“Thank God you believe me.”

“The evidence does point to this, but we are still investigating.”

“Let me show you exactly where the facility was,” Carlos says.

“We found it. Like I said, we found the chemical traces there too. The facility may no longer be there but the ground it sat on shows clearly that a building was there. The ground is disturbed,

leveled and packed down. It only has a loose covering to match the terrain but there was something built there. The shape is indicative of a large building."

"What about satellite pictures?" Carlos asks.

"I requested them but got back pictures of nothing here and the village abandoned. The same for the previous six months. Prior to that, however, they show the village."

"That is not possible."

"We know they were here recently. Photos are meant to deceive us into thinking they left long ago but the mass graves prove that the animals were buried recently."

"What next?" Carlos asks.

"What is next is we continue to investigate. Meanwhile, you need to go home. I promise I will keep you informed if you promise to let me do my job and not contact any more media."

"You were monitoring us?"

"It is my job. When you bring me an American military bolt and talk conspiracies, we watched you and people you associate with or knew. But I should not have to now, right?"

"No, of course not," Carlos assures him. "Thank you!"

"Okay, you are welcome to hang around. Just don't get in our way alright?"

"Thank you, sir. Can I call Eliza and tell her to stop?"

The colonel allows Carlos to make the call. After he has told Eliza to stop contacting the media, Carlos looks around and up at the stars piercing the evening sky. “Miguel, where are you?” he mutters to himself.

Stars Don't Lie

As Carlos is staring at the night sky as it creeps in, Miguel is witnessing the stars disappearing into the early morning. He makes his way back to his village and notices the mountain region appears strange."

"You are just now coming home?" Manuel asks and Miguel enters through the front door.

"Something is seriously wrong, Dad," Miguel says.

"The stars again?"

"The mountains too."

"What is wrong with the mountains?"

"They are not exactly right."

"They look alright to me."

"Dad, the mountains are the right ones but the ground is slightly different and the stars are in the wrong parts of the sky. We are in Australia."

"How come no one else shares your view?"

"I don't know why everyone does not see it. Stars don't lie, they show where we are and we are not in Mexico anymore."

"You need sleep, son. Get some and when you wake I will have some food laid out for you."

Miguel lays down and drifts off quickly. He wakes during the afternoon and the men are playing a game of sticks which involves taking a stick and knocking around rock around much like a hockey game on dirt. He smiles and joins Sarah and Laura with the other non-playing villagers and spectates. The strangeness of the mountains and stars seem to drift away as he is preoccupied with the merriment of village life. He even cheers his dad on as Manuel and Zane battle for points. It is a fierce and dusty game as the villagers laugh and cheer. Finally, Zane lands the game point winning for his team.

Manuel puts his arm around Zane. "That was great," he tells him.

Zane replies with pride. "I thought you had me there for a moment."

Miguel looks on with happiness his concerns forgotten. What does anything matter when there are good times like these? he thinks. At this moment the world seems right as the villagers share special sweet bread and share stories with each other. The fiesta carries on to the late evening as the stars break out and Miguel looks up and is again reminded they are not in the right place.

Stars Don't Lie

Hector yells out, "Well, Miguel, the stars still wrong?"

"The stars don't lie," Miguel replies.

Later that night as everyone turns in Miguel goes quietly to his bed and stares through the hole in his ceiling. Manuel looks up at his son wishing he could convince him that everything is all right.

"Ma'am, the dosage has been reduced as directed and we still have stable acceptance of the environment," the soldier reports to Jill that same evening.

"Very good. What about the boy?" she asks.

"He still questions where they are but seems more withdrawn now."

Jill stares at the monitor as the lights dim out in the village one by one.

"They had a good day of fun today," the scientist reports.

"Good. They deserve it." Jill walks back to her dorm room to sleep.

The next morning, Jill gathers the reports and meets with the director.

"We had a good day yesterday," she tells Charles. "We are almost down to no drug usage now and they are still accepting the environment variables. Also, they had a day of games and enjoyment."

“What about that boy?” Charles asks.

“He is falling in line with the others.”

“He still questions where they are?”

“Yes, but his questioning is lessening. I think he is adjusting well now.”

“Are you sure?”

“Absolutely, his irritation levels which are attributed to childhood reaction to the drug are almost non-existent. Now he is back to being a normal child.”

“Alright, good. We have a short time before they go back and need this to go smoothly.”

“There is no problem right now or in the foreseeable future, sir.”

Jill stands and smiles as she leaves. Charles seems skeptical but accepts her resolve.

Several days have passed and back in Mexico Carlos calls Colonel Garza. “Mr. Garza do you have any news?”

“Mr. Ortiz the government’s position seems to be that there is no concern. I have even reached out to some contacts in the USA military and nothing there either.”

"You know something is very wrong here. What can we do about it?"

"Mr. Ortiz, there is not much I can do my end until I get solid proof of where these people are. However, you are a private citizen. You might make as much noise about it as possible. At this point, it might shake something loose somewhere."

"I can guarantee you I will. However, I thought you did not want any publicity?"

"Sir, sometimes things cannot be solved by a military solution but requires the action of private citizens using a system of free communication to stir the pot. I will send a runner to your place with a file. It will be non-descriptive of our investigation but give you some good evidence to give to whoever you talk to. I wish you luck, Mr. Ortiz."

"Thank you, Colonel."

Later that day a plainclothes soldier gives Carlos a file with satellite pictures, ground readings of where the facility used to be and pictures of the village.

Carlos invites Eliza over to share the news. "I have something to show you," he tells her as she arrives. He shows her the file.

"Oh wow, Carlos, this is damaging evidence," she says as she flicks through the pages. "The military gave this to you just like that?"

“Yes, I think they themselves are being stonewalled and are at a loss as to what they can do. The colonel seems like a good man and wants to help. He asked us to reach out to the media with this stuff. Do you still want to help me?”

Eliza looks at the papers. “You better believe it.” Carlos smiles as they plan their media strategy.

Children Should be Seen Not Heard

Miguel seems more distant and withdrawn each day and his dad grows increasingly concerned.

"I don't know what to do about Miguel," he tells Sarah eventually, needing to confide in someone.

"He still worried about the star stuff?" she asks.

"Yes, he is insistent that we are in the wrong place."

"Maybe it is part of growing up. I know Laura has weird ideas at times."

"It is more than that. He is truly convinced we are in Australia. I could just kill my brother for filling his head with this stuff."

"Maybe his head is right."

"You don't believe him too, do you?"

"Look, I don't know anything about stars but I know when someone is troubled and feel they are right. Just like his dad."

"Dad?" Manuel repeats, looking at her.

"Yes, you do the same thing."

"I did not know you were that observant of me."

She laughs. "I have watched you for years."

Manuel leans over and kisses her. "I'm sorry," he says with a smile.

"Don't apologize for doing the right thing."

She leans over and he kisses her again.

Laura runs in. "Mommy can I play with Miguel?" she asks and they turn away quickly.

"Of course, he probably would like that," Sarah replies trying not to blush.

Manuel smiles. "I guess I need to get back to it."

Sarah nods okay as he walks away. She sits and continues her sewing hoping she has ruined nothing between them.

Laura runs over to Miguel sitting on his favorite rock staring at the ground. "What you doing, Miguel?" she says.

"Nothing," he replies.

"Why are you so down?"

"No one believes me that we are not in Mexico."

"That is so weird, Miguel."

"See, even you don't believe me."

"How do you know?"

Miguel looks at her and says, "It does not matter."

"It matters."

He looks back up a little encouraged at her attention. "You see, Laura, the stars don't lie. They are constantly where they should be in the sky. They move as the Earth turns but at certain times of the year, all the stars should always be in their rightful place. Right now, the Southern Cross which is a constellation – you know what a constellation is?" She shakes her head so he explains. "It is a bunch of stars in a group. Like a village of stars. They live together and form a person, animal or thing. The Southern Cross forms across that is visible in the bottom half of the Earth. However, the Southern Cross should be over there at this time of year." Miguel points to part of the sky and then points to another. "It is over there now, in the wrong place. It and other stars tell me we are in Australia which is on the other side of the Earth from Mexico. Do you understand?" She nods, intently listening to him.

After explaining in detail what he knows, Laura says, "I wish you were my brother."

"Why?"

"You and your dad always seem to take care of me and mommy."

Miguel looks at her staring at the ground and puts his arm around her. "You know what? I will be your brother," he tells her with a smile.

She returns his smile then hears her mom calling her.

"I got to go."

Miguel nods as she runs off back home, continuing to doodle in the dirt a map of the world.

Laura runs into her home. "Mommy, we are in Australia," she announces.

"You are convinced too, are you?"

"You don't believe Miguel? Stars don't lie, he says."

"I believe he is convinced he is right, but I am not sure."

They sit down to eat as Laura asks, "Mommy, can Miguel be my brother? He said he would be when I asked him."

Sarah is a little embarrassed. "He does take care of you, doesn't he?"

"Just like his dad takes care of you."

"Yes, sometimes." They continue eating and thinking about their relationships.

That evening Sarah asks Manuel to walk with her. She holds his hand and as he looks at her she smiles up and him.

"I want you to consider something okay?" she says.

"Of course."

"What if Miguel is right and we are not in Mexico anymore?"

"What?"

"Just hear me out. Do you know anything about stars?" Manuel shakes his head. "Well, Miguel does and he knows a lot. I am thinking he may be right."

"Maybe right?"

"Actually, I believe him."

"Why?"

"Because he knows what he is talking about. He spends his nights looking at those stars, how could he be so wrong?"

"I don't agree. I think it is an attention thing."

"Really, Manuel? Look I am not your wife and can't tell you anything about your son, but I am telling you that you need to listen to him."

"Look I know you are fond of me and him, but siding with my son is no way to try to gain favor with me."

"Is that what you think this is? I am telling you that your son is right and you think it is a game I am playing with you?"

"I am sorry. I'm just not sure why this is so important."

"It is important because your son is right and we are in the wrong place."

"Well, I do not agree and fancy science talk is not going to convince me we are on the other side of the world. Look if we are, how did we get here? Did space creatures move us?"

"I don't know, but I do know he is right and I think you are just being stubborn not wanting to believe him."

"I believe my son when he is right."

"I think you are so wanting things to be normal, you will ignore anyone, including me and your son. People that love you don't try so hard to convince you of things you know."

"How can you be so certain Miguel is right?"

"Because my heart cares for him and wants to believe him. Laura believes him and as his dad, you should believe him. He needs you to believe in him."

Sarah runs off back to the village as Manuel stares at her, astonished. He walks back and notices his son leaving his favorite rock in the distance and walking back to the village. As the night covers the land he stops and looks up at the stars. It looks as vague to him as to anyone not knowing patterns of nature. He walks back slowly pondering the issues of what disturbs the people in his life.

Manuel enters his home and Miguel is already in bed.

Children Should be Seen Not Heard

"Don't you want to eat, Miguel?"

"Not hungry, Dad," Miguel replies.

"You know Miss Martincz seems to agree with your Australia theory."

Miguel makes no reply to Manuel continues, "Look, son, the ground is the same isn't it?"

"Yes, it is," Miguel admits.

"Well then, how can the ground be right but the stars not?"

Manuel is about to leave when Miguel stops him. "Dad," he says. "How can we know where we are if all we do is look at the ground?" he asks.

Manuel looks at him with a strange expression and lowers his head to leave.

Later that evening when everyone has turned in and the village is quiet with slumber, Miguel is awoken by his dad whispering, "Miguel."

"Dad?"

"Son, gather some water and bread."

"Why?"

"We are leaving under the cover of darkness to check out this facility and why we are not in Mexico anymore."

Miguel smiles. "Yes, sir!"

"Quiet now. We need to meet Zane and a few villagers waiting at the main animal pen. No talking okay? Get your binoculars"

"Yes, sir."

They quietly walk to the animal pen where Zane and about ten villagers including Sarah and Laura are. They crouch below the height of the goats as they talk in the middle of the animals.

"We go in five groups of two," Manuel says. Everyone takes two animals with them and head off in various directions. Miguel and I will go towards the facility. I noticed something with your binoculars earlier when I hiked out there. Your binoculars pick up some kind of light beam that we can't see normally. I am guessing those beams alert them of people approaching and the animals will be a good distraction. We will approach the facility then let the animals go for them to think that is triggering the sensors. Then we will try to get in."

"That sounds very dangerous," Sarah whispers.

"It might be but we can't stay here. Who knows what they have in store for us next."

"You are right," Sarah admits.

"Everyone ready?" The people whisper yes and start with several goats. Manuel looks at Miguel. "You ready, son?"

"Completely."

They both grab their goats and head out towards the facility stopping occasionally to check for beams of light. They work around some gaps in the lights till they get to the facility where solid beams all around it.

"As soon as we pass through beams, we go quickly and low to the fence on the side. Then let the goats go as soon as they check it out. I am guessing they will come out and have to open the gate so we will enter then. Got it?" Manuel says.

"Got it."

They make it to the beam and break through it running to the fence trying to keep their profile hidden by the goats. As they make it to the fence a jeep starts up and then another. As they approach the fence it opens to let the jeeps out. Exiting the fence, Manuel releases the goats who immediately run off toward the village, the jeeps giving chase.

"Come on, they will be back very soon most likely," Manuel urges and he and Miguel run to the gate already starting to close. They make it in and put their backs to the wall. They are in-between the building wall and barrels and palettes of boxes. They make it around to the back corner and see the platform with a helicopter parked on it, two men in military uniforms stand guard talking. Manuel, who understands English, makes out they are not

on alert, it is just the goats that have disturbed their evening. Noticing the back door is open they sneak past the guards into the building.

They meander through halls looking into rooms which are empty and mostly dark. Not reading the signs in English they just keep searching and finally they find a large office that is open – it is the office of Jill Chambers. They see pictures of their village, villagers and themselves on her desk. Manuel accidentally knocks her computer keyboard and the computer screens light up showing camera views of their village and around the facility. They see the jeeps coming back and realize they must discover quickly these people.

Suddenly the bathroom door opens and Jill steps out. "Oh my God." She then speaks in Spanish. "How did you get in here?"

"We sneaked in," Manuel admits.

Jill runs over to her office door and locks it. "How in the world did you get past the sensors?"

"We used goats to distract you."

"I have to get you out of here," Jill says. "The people I work for are dangerous."

"Why did you move us to Australia?"

Jill cracks a big smile. "You are so smart, Miguel."

"You know our names?"

"I know everything about all of you. Look we don't have a lot of time because the sun will be coming up in an hour."

"We need to get back to Mexico," Manuel tells her.

"That is going to be a little hard. The fact is if you go back to your village and pretend none of this is happening you will be back there in a few weeks. We have to send you back before the season changes. You will know for sure something is wrong because the wrong season is changing from Mexico."

"Did you take Mr. Torres?" Miguel asks.

"Donkey, I mean Raul is here, under sedation."

"What is sedation?"

"He is sleeping, we gave him something to send him to sleep," Jill says.

"Were you going to return him?" Manuel asks.

"Yes, when we take you all back to Mexico."

"I don't believe you."

"It is true, I am the assistant director here."

"You know why I don't believe you?" Manuel says.

"Why?"

"My brother is surely looking for us by now."

"I know he is," Jill tells him. "He has been telling the story of you all missing on TV."

"Then how can you return us if we are missing and it is known?"

Jill stands back and covers her mouth. "You're right. Oh my God, you are right. They can't return you, not with that kind of attention. We have to get you out of here."

"We have to get Raul first," Manuel says.

"We can't chance it. We need to get you and Miguel out of here."

"We can't leave Mr. Torres."

"Okay, I'll show you where to go," Jill says.

"You will risk your life for us?" Miguel asks Jill.

"Yes, I would. Maybe we can all get out of this together." She goes to her desk to look at the computer monitors and quietly escorts them to a lab nearby, unlocking the door with a keypad. Inside, Raul is lying on the table with an IV in his arm. Jill removes the IV and Manuel picks him up and puts him over his shoulder. They wait for her at the door as she plugs a video cable into a black box causing the cameras in the infirmary to scramble.

"It will take them about fifteen minutes to figure out what is wrong with the video," she tells them and leads them down the hall to the outside.

"Get in that jeep under the tarp and I will be back in a few seconds. I need to grab the keys." As she goes back into the building as Manuel sits Raul in the back of the jeep and unfolds a tarp. He looks over but Miguel is not next to him.

"Miguel," he whispers urgently. Miguel finally runs up and clambers into the jeep. They cover up as daylight arrives.

"I have to leave here like normal so be quiet as I talk to the gate control person," Jill whispers to them. "We are going to leave the reservation completely and try to make it to the town nearby. The problem is going to be the helicopter."

"I took care of it, ma'am," Miguel tells her.

Jill looks over and Miguel has chained the helicopter undercarriage to the fence.

"Smart little guy," she says with a smile and climbs into the driver's seat and starts the jeep. "ID and code please?" the gate controller asks.

"Jill Chambers Assistant Director 796344 requesting exit access to check project village outskirts."

"Verified, yes ma'am. We are having some video problems."

The gates open as she replies, “That is why I need to visually check the villagers.”

“Have a good one, ma’am,” the gate controller says.

Jill slowly leaves and goes down the trail that winds far around to the north of the village. Once out of the view of the facility she guns the jeep as fast as she can.

“Okay, guys you can come out. No point in hiding now, as soon as the videos are up they are going to know what is going on,” she yells at her.

Manuel and Miguel uncover from the tarp and grab onto the roll bars of the jeep. Raul lays catatonic on the jeep bed.

Meanwhile, in the facility security have called the director to report on the issues with the monitors.

“This crap again,” Charles growls as he enters the security room.

“Usually a restart of the system fixes it but not coming up now. Jill left a few minutes ago to visually inspect the villagers,” one of the security guards tells him.

“Hmm, okay. Was there a problem?” Charles asks.

“None she told us about.”

"Typical."

Another tech comes into the control room. "Sir, we have a problem. Test subject thirteen is gone."

"Subject thirteen?" Charles says.

"Donkey, the villager we captured. He is not in the infirmary and the video lead was plugged into itself so I fixed it. Should be coming back live any moment."

The cameras come back on-line just in time for Charles to see a dust trail down the facility road.

"Zoom in on that vehicle," Charles orders.

The controller zooms in and they see the jeep's occupants. "Oh my God!" Charles exclaims. "Code 179 shutdown and pursue!"

The technician gets on the microphone and pages everyone in the facility as strobes and buzzers sound out. "This is a code 179. We have subjects and Jill Chambers trying to escape the reservation."

Outside the facility, guards storm out and get into jeeps to chase down the escapees. The helicopter pilot sees his helicopter chained to the fence and screams, "Get me a cutting torch!"

Jeeps are in pursuit as the villagers can see the dust commotion far in the north and eventually the helicopter taking off in the distance.

"Go, gentlemen, go," Hector says. Villagers hold each other in heightened anticipation of what will happen. They know the game has ended.

Jill is driving as fast as she can and nears the reservation gates.

"Secure the gate," Charles orders.

"Ma'am look!" Manuel yells and Jill sees three metal posts rising up in front of the main gate entrance.

"Everyone hang on tight!" she shouts and veers off the road crashing through the fence away from the gate and bouncing back onto the road heading towards town. Manuel keeps looking back and can see the helicopter approaching and the jeeps in the distance.

Jill speeds through the few traffic lights on the outskirts of a small Australian city and the commotion of her jeep with two other vehicles giving chase causes a lot of attention. She stops abruptly in front of two cop cars present at an accident. The cops turn quickly and take position defensively as Jill raises her hands.

"I am an American research scientist at the nearby government reservation. I have three Mexican nationals that are being held prisoner by people I work for. We need your protection now."

Children Should be Seen Not Heard

One cop gets on his radio. “Sir, you better come over to Victoria Street, we have an unusual situation here.” He sees the two other jeeps arrive and the helicopter overhead hovering in the distance. “You might want to bring back-up,” he adds.

The cops walk over to the jeep and look at Jill and her passengers. The pursuing vehicles have stopped nearby and one technician approaches.

“Hello there, officer. I am Sergeant Tiler from the American operations unit and these are mental patients currently being treated at our facility. Our employee here is suffering from a breakdown and kidnapped these people from our care. We apologize for the issue and will escort them back to our base now.”

“Hold on there, Sergeant. Nobody is going anywhere till we straighten this out,” the cop tells him.

“We are under government mandate and license to operate here and I would advise not interfering in an international incident.”

Charles is listening in from the guard’s microphone and watching the helicopter camera monitoring the situation. “Do we have another jeep?” he asks. “I need to get out there.”

Police back-up arrives including the chief of police driving to work when he heard the call.

"What is going on here?" he asks his colleague.

"Sir, this lady drove up to us claiming these men are being held prisoner at an American facility at that base nearby and she busted them out. She is seeking asylum with us. The guards in black there claim they are mental patients and she is suffering from some kind of breakdown and has abducted them. They are trying to take them all back citing international treaty."

The facility sergeant approaches the chief. "Sir, this is a very delicate matter and does not, with all due respect, involve any local police. Our director is on his way here now and should be here any minute."

"Good because there is a lot of explaining to be done. Meanwhile you men will relinquish your arms to my officers right now," the chief of police demands.

"Sir, we are authorized to carry firearms as per our charter with your government."

"I am sure, but not in my town," the chief says.

"Give up your weapons, men," the facility sergeant says, reluctantly. All the guards disarm and stand aside as Charles drives up.

Children Should be Seen Not Heard

"Sergeant, why are you not back with our people on the reservation?" Charles demands.

"Are you in charge of this operation?" the chief of police asks, walking over to Charles.

"Yes, sir, I am. Charles Tanner director of operations."

"You mind explaining all this to me, Mr. Tanner, director of operations?"

"I don't have time really, we need to go. I am not at liberty to discuss details."

"I see. Well, my advice is that you'd better declassify this right now and tell me."

Charles stands staring as the chief gives him a deadpan look. "Alright," he concedes, "these people are employees of our facility. Jill is my assistant director and she has taken three patients we have brought there to treat."

"Treat? What is wrong with them?" the chief asks.

"They have a rare condition and need to be isolated," Charles told him.

"Isolated? Are they contagious?"

"Could be," Charles says.

Jill speaks up. "Sir, he is lying. They are prisoners of a secret relocation project. They are not Americans but native Mexicans brought here to test the project."

"Not true, sir," Charles says.

The chief walks up to Manuel. "Do you understand, sir?" Manuel shrugs his shoulders as the chief says, "Habla?"

Manuel shakes his head and says a few Spanish phrases.

"This is a serious medical issue and we need to take them back to isolation right now," Charles insists.

The chief looks at Charles then back at Manuel, Raul sleeping and then Miguel.

"Habla?" he says to Miguel who utters one word in response, "Stars."

The chief smiles at Miguel then he turns around to Charles. "These are not patients. Since when do Americans treat Mexicans in Australia for anything? If they are contagious, why are you people not in bio-suits? Officers arrest all these people."

The police arrested the guards as Charles is handcuffed. "You are making a career mistake here. This is a sanctioned operation by both our governments," Charles tells the chief.

The chief walks up to Jill and her passengers and yells back to Charles, "Tell it your people then!" Looking at Jill he says, "Are you alright, ma'am?"

Jill sheds a tear. "You just saved our lives, sir, literally."

"Ma'am, I may not know anything about clandestine government projects but I know when people are in mortal danger. I don't know what kind of operation this is you are doing but to risk your job and maybe life to bring these people here proves something was up. Officers take them to my office and don't allow anyone near them unless I authorize it."

"Thank you, sir."

"Dónde estoy?" Raul murmurs as he wakes up.

"What did he say? the chief asks.

"He is wondering where he is," Jill explains.

Jill tells Manuel, Miguel and Raul they will be safe now and to follow her. The police cart away guards and Charles as the helicopter flies back to the facility. The chief tells his officers, "Leave a team here to watch that gate in case more soldiers come. If anyone not Australian comes near here, arrest them."

Exposed

Jill is at police headquarters explaining the whole project and what they have been doing on the reservation next to the chief's town.

One of the police officers pokes his head around the door. "Sir, that director Charles fellow is demanding to call his people."

"Tell him he gets no calls, and I have already notified our government so they will talk to his ambassador." He focuses back on Jill. "So you are saying there are more people on that base held hostage?"

"Yes, chief."

The phone rings and the receptionist tells the chief that Sheila Sommers is on the phone.

"Yes, ma'am. No, ma'am that did not happen. That is correct, ma'am, we did disarm and arrest them. Yes, I am sure they are. I understand."

"That sounded scary," Jill says as the chief hangs up the phone.

"That was the prime minister of Australia and she is sending your ambassador along with some of our military here to handle this. I am sorry, I am not sure what will happen but it is out of my hands now."

"I understand," says Jill, looking nervous.

The chief takes Jill back to the recreational room with Miguel, Raul and Manuel being looked at by local doctors.

"How are you guys doing?" Jill asks them in Spanish.

"What will happen to us and my village?" Manuel asks.

"I'm not sure. The military for Australia is on their way to take over." She looks at Miguel. "How are you doing, Miguel?"

"I feel like I should have ignored the stars," he says.

"Don't feel that way, Miguel. You did an incredibly brave and smart thing. No matter what happens, you will be remembered for what you did. I promise you."

Miguel smiles.

Hours pass and the chief asks his officers watching the gate and reservation if they have witnessed any activity.

"No, sir, it is quiet over there, nothing moving anywhere," the guard reports.

"Keep watching, it will be tomorrow before the military gets here. I have officers coming regularly to relieve you guys soon.

Exposed

The military will arrive and take over the area. When that happens you can report back here."

"Yes, sir."

The next day the military shows up.

"Chief of police Donald," the chief says, holding out his hand.

"Air Marshal Tom Jacks. Where are the American prisoners?"

"Which ones? Mine or theirs?"

"Yours."

The chief takes them to the holding cells

"About time you guys showed up," Charles says, standing from his bunk.

"This is Charles who is the director of this whole mess," the chief says, introducing him to the Air Marshal.

"Look, sir, do we not have the mandate to be here?" Charles asks the Air Marshal.

"Yes, sir, you do."

"Good. Can you then get these locals to release us and our patients so we can take them back to the reservation?"

"Your patients, as you call them, will not be going back with us to your base," the Air Marshal tells him

"What do you mean going back to our base? And what do you mean us?" Charles looks at the ambassador. "Tom, what is going on?"

“I have been given operation command to proceed onto your base and take over any and all facilities therein by order of the Prime Minister of Australia and by the President of the United States.”

“Dear God,” Charles says when he realizes the Air Marshal is serious.

“Your men will be placed under arrest and taken to our base for processing by your government. You will come with me and contact the remaining staff at your facilities to stand down and cease all activities. They will relinquish all weapons and you will escort my men there to take control. Your people are ordered to comply with helping us care and for the remaining hostages and providing all information needed to return them home.”

“Tom, do they understand we have a charter to run this operation?”

“Director, the operation has been canceled by President Newsome and she has executively ordered any and all Lazarus related projects be defunded and seized.”

The chief has his officer unlock the jail in front of Charles. “G’day mate,” the officer says and Charles steps out with a disgusted look at the big smile on the chief’s face.

Exposed

The chief takes the Marshal and Ambassador up to waiting room where Jill and the villagers are as the American guards and Charles are being released to military control.

“Ma’am this is Air Marshal Jacks who is now in charge of this situation,” he says to Jill.

“Ma’am under the authority of my government and the American government I am taking over your facility and care as well as the return of the villagers. You will assist us with your director to facilitate this change,” the Air Marshal says.

“That would be nice,” Jill replies.

“See it all works out,” the chief tells the Marshal before he takes his leave.

Thank you, gentlemen,” Jill says, with tears of relief in her eyes. She turns and speaks in Spanish to Manuel and Miguel. Their eyes light up and they smile.

Jill turns to the Marshal. “Sir, this is the young man that realized they were not in Mexico anymore by looking at the stars. He and his father Manuel broke into our facility and found me. I bought them and Raul back.” Miguel looks at Jill recognizing the word stars. The Marshal walks up to Miguel and says as Jill translates: “It is an honor to meet a bright and brave young man.”

Miguel smiles and sees the medals on the Marshal’s uniform. He points to one ribbon with a medal with a cross and star. “Que es

como la constelación de la cruz del sur, e incluso tiene una estrella en ella," he says and the Marshal looks to Jill for translation.

"Sir, he said your medal has a cross like the Southern Cross constellation and even has a star in it."

"That, young man, is the Distinguished Service Cross I was given for providing support in a remote country called Afghanistan helping US forces. We freed a town that had been held hostage by hostile forces in the region."

Jill translates and as Miguel smiles, the Marshal unpins his Service Cross and pins it on Miguel saying, "Now it goes to a better man who did the same but for his own people."

Miguel looks at the medal then looks up at his dad. Manuel smiles back at his son's pride. The Marshal steps back and salutes Miguel.

The Marshal and his soldiers take Jill, Miguel, Manuel, Raul outside to join Director Charles to see the American base.

"You have no idea what you have done," Charles hisses at Jill.

"I did the right thing, Charles, it is not about us anymore."

"Violet will not stand for this!" Charles replies angrily.

Exposed

The Marshal chips in. "I suggest, sir, you keep your opinions to yourself for the remainder of your stay in our great country."

"I have rights, sir," Charles demands.

The Marshal stands in front of Charles. "We will see about your rights after we see what rights you stepped on with these people, comprende?"

The Marshal escorts Charles, Jill and the villagers, along with a very large contingent of military vehicles and soldiers. The city police have left watching the city outskirts having been relieved by Australian soldiers. They salute as the caravan of military vehicles pass.

"Men stand down and follow us back to the compound," Charles tells his men. Everybody gets in their vehicles and drive to the base compound where they are confronted by guards and scientists outside. Charles steps out and says to everyone, "This facility is now under Air Marshal Jacks' control. We are ordered by the President to comply with any and all commands given by him and his men. All guards will disarm and safety all weapons. This operation is halted." The director then escorts the Marshal, villagers, and Jill into the operations room.

"My God what are you people doing?" the Marshal asks as he sees the video monitors trained on the village. "You have been introducing drugs into their water supply?" he asks, seeing the paperwork on the director's desk.

"This is an important project in case there is a need to relocate third world people to a more habitable and suitable environment," Charles tells him.

The Marshal looks at Charles with disbelief. "You think I got to this rank because I am stupid? This is about relocating people to exhume resources they happen to be near. If you want to help people, help build farms, habitats where they live. What you are doing here is wrong. Where were you planning to take these people? To my country permanently?"

"They were going back to their homeland in several weeks," Charles admits quietly.

The Marshal turns and looks at the facility monitors and then turns to Jill almost in tears.

"I believe you were going to take them back home but not alive. How could you? They would tell all when they got back. No, I think you were going to kill them off in some pandemic, poison water well or something. Weren't you?"

He looks at Charles as Charles looks away. "That is what I thought. No, sir, you are not doing science here, it is evil, just plain evil. What scares me is this was just a test pilot for something else. I just hope when your country's justice system gets a hold of you,

they make you spill it all publicly." The Marshal walks up to Charles. "I am so tempted to make you tell us right now what this was leading up to. Believe you me, I could get it out of you. But I won't, you have rights although you do not deserve them." The Marshal turns again to the monitors. "I promise you this. I don't care what country you come from or who you really represent. If your people ever come to my country and do anything like this again, you will find me leading an assault on your facility and your people will not like it. You take that back to your superiors," the Marshal tells Charles and orders his men to start to shut down the facility and process the workers to the proper authorities in their country.

The villagers watch as they see jeeps approaching from both sides. One jeep stops in front and Miguel, Manuel and Donkey clamber down and run to meet them. Manuel and Sarah hug and stare at each other as they kiss. Miguel and Laura look at their parents and smile at each other.

Jill steps forward and says in Spanish, "People this is the Air Marshal for Australia and he is liberating this town from an evil plot to keep you here."

"Manuel, what is going on here? We really are in Australia?" Hector says.

"Listen, everyone. We were abducted by some people that wanted see if they could fool us by moving us. Jill worked with them but turned and helped Miguel and Manuel, as well as Raul, leave. We are in Australia and only my son, Miguel, had the brains to figure it out." Manuel puts his hand on Miguel's head and looks down at his son. "I am so proud of you," he says.

"Miguel saved us?" Hector asks.

"Yes," says Manuel.

The villagers gather around Miguel to congratulate him. Hector steps out to Jill and asks, "What happens to us now?"

Jill translates as the Marshal says, "You will be returned to your home. The government of Mexico has already been investigating your disappearance and is preparing to receive all of you back."

"What about our dead?" Hector says.

"I am sure they will take care of that," Jill tells him.

"It will take a couple of days to get you back, but we will be here with you and you will be well taken care of as guests of my country," the Marshal tells them.

"Thank you," Jill says after translating this to the villagers.

"Thank you," Manuel repeats in English.

Exposed

Marshal smiles and shakes his hand.

"What will happen to you?" Manuel asks Jill.

Jill looks down. "I am going to jail because I was a part of this. That does not matter as long as you all are okay."

"That is not right for you to go to jail. You saved us."

"It is alright."

Hector looks at Miguel and sees the Marshal's medal. "Little man what is that on your shirt?" he asks.

Miguel looks at the medal. "The Marshal gave it to me. It is a war medal he wanted me to have."

"Well, you earned it," Hector tells him and walks over to the Marshal to shake his hand. "Sir, thank you for taking care of us and for giving that boy your medal."

"Yes, sir, it was my honor to give that young man something for his courage. For what he has done will open the eyes of the world to something very big. To recognize what he did and try to help his village at his age, that is huge. That is what a true hero is all about." The Marshal salutes as Hector nods.

Everything settles down as the soldiers bring in food and supplies for the villagers. Some villagers play games with the soldiers as they have brought in their own translators.

“Ma’am, it is time for you to go,” the Marshal tells Jill. “Charles and most of his team are at our base by now in the process of being handed over to your government.”

“I understand. Let me say goodbye to the villagers.”

“Of course, ma’am.

Jill walks up to Manuel and kisses him on the cheek. “I have to go now,” she says.

“I want you to stay with us,” Miguel tells her.

“I want to as well but I have to go. Maybe someday I will see you again.”

“Promise?” says Miguel.

“I promise,” Jill replies.

The villagers wave goodbye to Jill as she leaves in the jeep with the Marshal and key staff. As they leave the village back to the road leaving the reservation they fall behind military vehicles carrying items from the facility including the helicopter. As they approach the main gate she sees the partially repaired fence she took down.

“You made a nice hole there I hear,” the Marshal says.

“Not bad for my first breakout,” Jill admits with a smile.

“May I ask you something between you and me?”

"Of course."

"Obviously someone of great influence with the capability to use your and my government resources built this. Who would this be, do you think?"

"I really don't know that much about them but they are a very powerful family, I believe. I know Charles was scared of them."

"Hmmm," the Marshal says thoughtfully. He stares out at the skyline as they approach the outskirts of the city. "You know this is likely to be whitewashed in your country and you might not survive this?"

Jill stares at the Marshal as he looks at her. She looks out at the horizon and says, "It does not matter as long as the villagers are safe."

"You did a good thing here ma'am. No matter what, you will be remembered for it," the Marshal tells her.

Jill cries as they drive off to the base.

A New Day Arises

After a long and exhausting day, the villagers sleep well having been fed a lot of food and from overall relief after the confusion. As morning breaks they are greeted by soldiers that have prepared a breakfast feast for them all. Doctors and psychologists continue to question and monitor the villagers.

Hector talks to Manuel as he picks up some dirt and rocks. "They really had us fooled," he says.

"We had no idea," Manuel agrees. "They tell me that we were given drugs to help accept that we were not home anymore."

"I don't understand how drugs can keep you from knowing where you are."

"Apparently there are drugs like that and a lot of other things we don't know about," Manuel says.

"What is to keep them from doing this again?"

Manuel smiles. "We have Miguel who will always check the stars."

"Yes, we do," Hector says with a laugh.

"Mr. Ortiz."

Manuel looks up to see Sarah standing next to him. "Ms. Martinez."

"Excuse me, I am needed elsewhere," Hector says and departs.

"You know, Mr. Ortiz, that was very brave what you did back there," Sarah says.

"It was dumb and lucky."

"It was brave and good," Sarah insists.

"I need to learn to listen to people better."

"You did listen to people."

"I need to tell people what I feel about them."

"Maybe they know how you feel about them."

"I love you, Sarah."

"I know, Manuel."

Manuel and Sarah stare at each other. "I know you love me and I love you very much. You are the bravest man I could ever love," Sarah says.

"Will you be my wife?" Manuel asks.

"More than anything in the world."

They kiss for the longest time and then hug. A soldier slowly walks up. "Sorry, excuse me, ma'am. Sir, we are ready to deploy in the morning. This will be your last night here. I have already informed the rest of the villagers."

A New Day Arises

"Thank you," Manuel says. The soldier walks off as Manuel looks at Sarah. "We are going home."

Sarah smiles and kisses him. "I will make it a better home than it was before. Now give me another kiss while we are in Australia.

"What's wrong?" Sarah asks eventually, seeing Manuel looking around.

"It is a beautiful country you know, it looks similar to home but it's strange. Now I know, it is so obviously not our country, but it is a beautiful place. I am ready to go home though."

"It does not matter where we are as long as we are together," Sarah says with a smile.

They walk up to the villagers all starting to prepare for the move in the morning. Soldiers help pack belongings in plastic boxes carefully as if each thing in the village is a priceless item.

"Children, we have something to tell you," Manuel says and Miguel and Laura approach. "We are going to be married. Son, you are about to have a sister."

"Mom, really?" says Laura.

"Yes, love."

Laura looks at Miguel. "You are going to be my brother. Oh boy!"

Miguel laughs. "Come on then, sister, let's look around this place one last time."

"Not too late, we are leaving early," Manuel shouts after them.

Later that night, Miguel sits on his Aussie rock staring at the stars as Laura watches with him.

"The stars are beautiful," Laura observes.

"They are the greatest things that God has ever made," Miguel says.

"Will you teach me what they mean?"

Miguel looks at Laura. "Of course, sister."

"You know, I am going to like you calling me that. I will still stick my tongue out at you though.

"Guess it is time for me to go back," Laura says, hearing Sarah call. Sarah calls her again and several soldiers yell her name too, laughing. Laura walks. "I can't wait to get home."

Laura runs off as Miguel keeps looking at the stars for a while. When he eventually returns to the village, a soldier, "Oy, are we still in Australia?"

"Yes, sir," Miguel replies.

"Just checking because you are the only one that would know that."

Miguel smiles and goes to his house.

"Back already, son?" Manuel says.

A New Day Arises

"I have seen enough tonight and I'm ready to see the stars in our sky."

"Amen."

They eat a little something and prepare for bed.

"Dad, will this happen again?" Miguel asks.

"One of the soldiers told me that our government is going to check on us regularly to make sure it does not."

"That is good. I am still going to look at the stars each night just to make sure."

"Please do."

They both chuckle as they drift off to sleep.

The News

Eliza is in her apartment watching the news of the villagers in Australia as the doorbell rings.

"Oh my God I just saw the news!" she exclaims when she sees Carlos standing there.

"The colonel just told me an hour ago and I ran over here to tell you."

Eliza jumps and hugs Carlos. "I am so relieved."

"It is a good day."

"Please come in. Can I get you a drink?"

"A tea would be nice."

"Perfect, I have some made." Carlos sits and watches the news playing as she brings two cups of tea and sits next to him."

"It did not take long for the media to catch the story," Carlos says.

"Well they were primed for it but just did not how to pursue the abduction. Guess they were still trying to investigate it when this hit."

They both listen to the TV reporter.

The villagers were relocated from their native country of Mexico onto a government leased land in Australian by a United

States contractor. The contractor was mandated by a business consortium to relocate this unwilling and unknowing small village. Sources in the Australian military tell us that a young boy who knew a lot about astronomy discovered they were in Australia and convinced his village to take action. Several villagers including the said young boy broke into the contractor's monitoring facility and rescued one of their own who was being held captive. They convinced a high-level contract official to help them escape and were chased to a nearby town. Police officials of the town seized the contractors and escapees and held them for Australian and American officials to decide what to do next.

"Miguel figured it out," Eliza says.

"Apparently he did. Way to go, my nephew."

Eliza holds up her cup in a toast. "Do you know when they will be back?" she asks Carlos.

"Colonel Garza said they are being processed and should be back in a matter of days. They are being medically cared for right now. Apparently, they had been drugged."

"Oh my God! Really?"

"They should be fine he said."

Eliza turns the volume down a little as they continue to drink and listen.

"It might seem strange to ask at this moment, but it just popped into my head," Carlos says.

"What is that?"

"Why did you not marry him?" Eliza looks at Carlos as he stares back. She gets up without saying a word.

"I am sorry, that was wrong of me to ask."

"No, you are fine," Eliza tells him. "Just give me one minute." She walks into her bedroom and comes back with a shoe box. She sits down next to Carlos and smiles. Turning to her box she unties a ribbon from around it. He sees letters he wrote to her and cards, but on top is a ring box which she hands to him. Carlos grabs the box with a confused look and opens it to find the ring he bought her.

"How…?" he asks, confused.

Eliza looks at the ring. "After the wedding and the annulment I went back to the restaurant we went to for my birthday and the waiter remembered me. Said we had left something valuable. He brought me the ring in the box and swore it had to be mine because we were the last people there that night at the table on which he found it. I looked at the ring and the style and I knew it came from you. I figured out what you must have been trying to do that night.

You wanted to propose to me. I kept the ring to always remember you."

"I never knew. Why did you not tell me?"

"I figured I had broken your heart and proved I was not patient enough to wait for you. At the time I thought you would never propose although I always hoped you would. I am in love with you, Carlos. Everything about you, your family in the village, your style, your life, but never thought you wanted to settle down."

"I never did, till I met you. I was just not brave enough to tell you. I would have that night at the restaurant but when you told me about your fiancé, I could not do it. Besides, I felt maybe it was better you went with Mr. Right."

"He was never Mr. Right, just Mr. Right Now. He was a distant second to you."

Carlos looks at the ring and back at Eliza whose eyes are sparkling. He gets down on one knee as her face becomes flushed. "Miss Eliza Gomez, would you marry me and make me the proudest man in the world?"

"Mr. Ortiz, I would be proud to be your wife."

Carlos puts the ring on her finger. "I love you, Eliza."

They both stand and kiss passionately. “I love you, Carlos. I have waited a long time for this,” Eliza says.

“Then this is truly a good day on all fronts,” Carlos replies with a smile.

The Journey Home

Early morning arrives and the soldiers make sure everyone is up to eat breakfast and prepare to leave. Travel buses arrive at the village to take everyone comfortably to the military base where an airline jet is awaiting them. The Marshal shows up to greet the villagers.

"Good morning, folks. In an hour after you have eaten and ready yourselves we will depart. Your belongings will be loaded by us and we will take care of everything. These buses behind me will transport each and every one of you to an airport where you will be flown back to Mexico. When you reach the base in Mexico you will be checked by officials of your country and then transported to your real village. Now the materials that make up your homes is here. It will be returned and placed back by the same people who moved it in the first place. It took them a while to do that the first time while all of you were in a drug-induced sleep. Since that is not going to happen again, it has been arranged by the US government for you all to stay in portable housing till your homes are rebuilt. And they will be rebuilt to whatever specification you want. If you want them exactly like you had before, that is what will happen. However, I would encourage you to accept the much better-built homes being offered as reparation

for your internment. You can pretty much ask for anything and it will be granted, I am told. So, on your way back, think very carefully about what you would like."

The Marshal paces around. "I can't imagine what life is like for you at this moment but I can assure you of this. I will devote myself to watching for this kind of behavior and making sure it never happens again. This reservation has been revoked by my government and no longer will be in the hands of people that ran it. I promise you that those that did this will pay dearly for it. God bless you all and good luck for the rest of your lives."

The Marshal walks up to Miguel and shakes his hand. "Young man, it is an honor. Take care of this village."

Miguel listens to the interpreter. "Si, sir," he says with a nod. The Marshal winks at Miguel and turns to leave.

Zane watches as soldiers carefully exhume his mom and place her in a casket-like container to preserve her for the journey. Manuel and Miguel stand next to him.

Zane looks over to Manuel and Miguel. "You know the strange thing? My mom always wanted to visit Australia. She never even knew she was here."

The Journey Home

Miguel grabs Zane by the shoulder. “We are going home, friend.”

“Thanks to you guys,” Zane says.

Miguel and Manuel go to gather their stuff while Zane watches as the soldiers load his mom’s casket onto the vehicle. “You will be home soon, mom,” he says.

Everything is loaded up and the villagers board the bus. Miguel looks back at his dad smiling with pride and happiness. The bus moves and everyone cheer before growing quiet as they pass through the gates of the reservation and head through the city. People of the city are standing on each side of the main street with the police looking like they are witnessing a parade. Cheering and wishes of good luck follow them and Miguel hears his name.

“Dad, do they know about me?” Miguel asks.

“The whole world knows about you,” one of the soldiers tell him.

“Wow,” says Miguel staring at the cheering crowds. Manuel and Sarah smile at each other.

The conversations on the bus turn to what kind of housing would they like.

“Should we rebuild with two houses or just one?” Sarah asks Manuel.

“Two.”

"Why two?"

"One for all of us and the other for your daughter to have when she is old enough," Manuel says with a smile.

"Okay, but what about Miguel?"

"I don't think he will be living with us long enough," Manuel says. "I think his path is going to take him elsewhere."

"He will do well no matter which part of the Earth he is on. He has proven that."

"Yes, he has," Manuel agrees.

After many hours they approach another larger city on the outskirts of the airforce base. As they approach, fireworks erupt in the night sky and people are celebrating in the streets. Police cars escort the caravan with their police lights on. Again, people are chanting Miguel's name. Thousands of people are cheering and chanting. They drive through the city and make it to the entrance of the airforce base where there is a large airline jet awaiting them on the tarmac. The caravan stops near the plane and soldiers assist the villagers to an escalator that takes them into the plane. Miguel's eyes are full of excitement seeing fireworks in the city behind them and his first plane ride he was conscious for.

The Journey Home

"This flight will take you to the airforce base in Mexico," the Marshal tells them. "Good luck to you all." The villagers listen to the interpreter and wave goodbye to the Marshal.

"Does anyone understand us since the interpreters left?" Manuel says.

"Yes, sir, we all understand you," a flight attendant tells him. "This is a Mexican airline you are on. It is a passenger jet but we are landing at a military base to ensure your safety back to your village. Can I get you anything?"

Manuel looks at Sarah. "We are good, thank you."

The plane grows quiet as people that have lived a simple life listen to the roar of a jet plane moving. Some are frightened but they all know it is necessary to get home. The plane makes it to the air and eyes stare out the windows looking at a city and country they knew little of. Miguel continues to watch the fireworks from the city as the jet flies away. As the plane approaches a high altitude they break through some clouds and Miguel sees a full moon glowing on the clouds making them look like cotton.

"Wow, how beautiful. Ma'am, how long till we reach Mexico?" he asks an attendant.

"Well, we have been flying for an hour so far, so that means we have around sixteen more hours to go."

"Like a whole day?" Miguel says.

"Correct, about 15 thousand kilometers."

“The Earth is 40 thousand kilometers around,” Miguel tells her.

“Smart boy, I did not know that,” the attendant says with a smile.

“It is shorter from north to south pole.”

“I see a future scientist here,” the attendant says and turns to deal with another passenger.

Miguel smiles as the attendant leaves. Laura is asleep as are several villagers slumbering through the repetitive roar of the plane. Miguel sees a magazine of astronomy in the seat in front of him. It is in English but has many pictures of the planets and astronomical telescopes around the world.

I want to visit these places, he thinks as he flicks through the magazine. After a while, the attendant walks by and sees Miguel sleeping, still holding the astronomy magazine when the plane bumps Miguel awake where he finds it is daylight.

“Have a good sleep, son?” his father asks.

“Yes, sir.”

“Hungry?” asks an attendant. “Breakfast is coming soon.

Time to Pay the Price of their Folly

Time to Pay the Price of their Folly.

While the villagers enjoy their long flight home Jill and Charles are already attending congressional hearings on the Lazarus project. Overseeing them is Senator Harrison who is aware he is in media and that the world is watching.

"Mr. Tanner and Ms. Chambers we have all read the reports and as you know this event has circled the globe as a shock is still penetrating all levels of power. Investigations are currently underway but we have already uncovered a number of players in this torrid game. I must say that as a 15-year senator I thought I had seen it all, but this really took the cake. I am astonished you actually thought you could get away with this. If it wasn't for Ms. Chambers finally doing the right thing, you might have. I hope Ms. Chambers you do not think that your change of heart at the last minute will constitute any immunity or leniency from this panel?"

"No, sir, I do not," Jill says. "I am as guilty as all the rest and accept my punishment. However, it was not me that put an end to it, it was Miguel, the boy from the village. If he had not convinced

his dad and the rest of the villagers that they had been abducted, and some of the villagers stealthily coming to raid the facility, I doubt I would have done anything. It was only when I saw them there, I knew I had to take action to save them."

"Yes, yes the boy is a hero for sure. I do respect that you have taken responsibility," the senator says.

"If I may say, sir, I am deeply sorry for being a part of it. There is no excuse for me. My regret is that I did not act sooner."

The room is quiet as Jill stares somberly at her table.

"May I say, sir," Charles adds, "that we were under orders in a mandate to do this government-sanctioned operation, so how can we be held responsible for doing our job?"

"Following orders has been the excuse for many atrocities in history, sir. You may be following orders but still must face the consequences of carrying them out. Do not soldiers die in battle following orders? Whether you are right or wrong in your actions, you accept the consequences of them following or giving the orders."

Charles looks around and sits back in his chair.

"Now then, Ms. Chambers, did the land these villagers live on have any resource of interest to this project?" the senator asks.

"Not really, sir, this was a test," Jill replies.

"So, this has never happened before?"

"No, sir, it has. We did it with homeless people in the US initially. It was very successful mainly to test the inhibiting drugs to disorient questioning of their location. Mexico was the next level because it was close by, a foreign land, and would answer the question that the project ultimately needed to answer."

"What was that question?"

"Could we successfully relocate multiple people from foreign soil without their government being aware of it, and move them to another foreign soil without that government being aware of it. Then would the people moved accept their new, yet similar, surroundings."

"And if they did, what then?"

"We would move to stage four which would be to move an indigenous group in a real target acquisition of resource."

"Wait a minute, stage four?" Harrison says. "What was stage one?"

"Stage one was a simple behavioral experiment disguised as a game called Lazarus. As you know that was stopped by Congress and our sitting president long ago. But it was meant to test behavior patterns and movement of people within various classes. This was important for the entire Lazarus project so we could

understand certain psychologies and later in tandem with certain synaptic inhibiting drugs."

"Where are these drugs made?"

"They are made by V pharmaceuticals," Jill says.

"Did these drugs go through the FDA in any way?"

"No, sir, they were not to be marketed in any way. They were funded through a government project code-named Purple. Only a select few knew of the plan and what was happening with it. Even the university that was working on the drug experiments only knew it was some kind of antipsychotic drug. However, it worked very well and was experimented on in various countries by their military on people who were paid subjects. When those results were measured and success had been obtained, we moved to stage two which was the homeless people."

"Why homeless people?"

"They are easy to access and are not kept track of by any group. They usually have no family or anyone that cares enough to be looking for them. Once the experiments were finished they were fed well, detoxed of all traces of our drug and then brought back to their original location."

"Do we know who they are?" Harrison asks.

Time to Pay the Price of their Folly

"Yes, we monitored them on and off for months afterward, just in case."

"In case of what?"

"Cognitive retention and drug side effects.

"Were there any side effects?"

"No, senator, the drug was 100% effective."

"My God. You didn't think to stop this then?"

"Actually I came in after this stage was completed. I was brought in for the stage three."

Harrison looks over at Charles. "And what stage were you brought in for?"

"Stage two," Charles replies.

"So you were there for the more deplorable start of this program?"

"It is not deplorable, it is a necessary program," Charles says.

"You really believe that?" the senator asks.

"Yes, sir."

"Interesting. Well you know everyone thinks they are right, even Hitler."

"I am not Hitler."

"Okay. Please explain the value of this program to me, then."

"What if long ago we could have moved Native Indians safely and without conflict saving thousands of lives?" Charles says. "If

we had the techniques then that we do now, we could enrich and save lives. In a modern world, there are limited resources which are needed to maintain the world. If a species of animal is living in an area that has those needed resources, we safely move their habitat so they can continue. A butterfly or monkey is not going to care where they live as long as it is familiar and it has plenty of food. I know it may seem strange but it is the reality of the world. How many lives – human and animal – have we destroyed building cities and even this very chamber in order to have what we have today?"

"That is very rational and I can understand how many people like you can come to that conclusion," Harrison admits. "However, let me expound my thinking on these matters. Yes, we can move animals and even plants to another location and do frequently with care. If the animal or vegetation does not naturally accept the new surroundings then they cannot be moved. We cannot invent chemicals to induce acceptance. Humans, on the other hand, have certain legal rights to live where they are. When you move them against their knowledge or will you have violated those rights. It does not matter if you make their life better afterward, especially if they did not agree to it with full understanding. I cannot speak for

our government of the past and about what happened to the Native Americans. I would say, why move them at all? If there is oil or some resource of value where they live then share it with them if they agree to allow its excavation. You see, sir, in a modern society we must find ways to come to agreeance with all peoples of all types and place in life. If they do not agree with our wishes to use their land then we move on. That is that! Do you understand that, sir?"

Charles stares ahead with a glassy look. Jill's head is down looking at the table as tears roll down her cheeks.

"Well, when the rights of others have been violated it is the job of those in charge like us to bring justice and make things right. So, someone is going to be moved against their will and that someone is you, sir. We will move you to a new location and we won't use drugs to do it. We will use law enforcement and incarceration to remove this kind of cancer from our society. If my colleagues have any questions or statements to make, please do so now."

The entire chamber is silent. Harrison looks around. "No? Okay. We will dismiss for today as my colleagues will confer to decide the outcome of what to do with all the players of this game."

Harrison bangs the gavel on the table and stands up as everyone murmurs and gets up to leave.

The following day the Senate hearings continue. Charles sits staring at the senators with contempt while Jill stares at the table in shame.

Harrison calls the session to order. "It is the opinion of this panel that Mr. Tanner and Ms. Chambers along with the workers and guards under their supervision will be taken to trial before a judge and jury. You will be under the indictment of kidnapping, murder, misuse of government resources, operating in an illegal capacity as a government agency, and violation of numerous human rights upon foreign soils. There will be other charges as well but you will hear them at your trials. You will be arrested and taken from this chamber to await trial. Ms. Chambers, I have personally vouched that you should face a lesser charge for your candid cooperation."

Jill is crying. "Yes, sir," she says through muffled sobs.

Charles has a stunned look on his face.

"Mr. Tanner believe me that everyone involved in this will face justice," Harrison says.

Time to Pay the Price of their Folly

The gavel strikes like a loud bell chiming their lives away. Police handcuff them both and take them to jail.

Home Again

The plane lands at a Mexico Airforce base. As it pulls onto the tarmac and the stairs pull in front, the villagers are escorted to the door. Miguel and Manuel are up front at the top of the stairs seeing numerous military people standing at attention as a band plays. They make their way down the stairs and are greeted by the president of Mexico and the US Ambassador to Mexico.

"Welcome home, young man," the president says, shaking Miguel's hand. He waves at everyone and repeats, "welcome home."

"On behalf of the United States, we are humbly thankful for your return and apologize for the actions of unsanctioned groups which at this moment are being brought to justice," the US ambassador tells them.

"Thank you, sir," Manuel says after hearing the translation.

A government official for the president steps forward. "The president is going to leave now but he wanted to welcome you back. If you will follow me, we will see to your immediate needs and if you would be a little more patient, we need to ask some questions about your ordeal and then send you to your homes."

The president smiles and waves as he leaves and the official escorts them to a cafeteria where they are served food before being individually questioned about events. After two hours they are placed back on the plane which has been refueled before being flown to an airport nearer to their homeland.

Eventually, the villagers land back in Mexico. After a few more hours by bus, they see the location of their old village in the distance. First, they pass the area where they first saw the facility and anticipation grow as they ascend the hill and see what remains of their village. There are electric lights and, as they approach, they see trailers lined up. Military vehicles and personnel are there to receive them. The area has been patrolled and visitors have been kept away to give the villagers peace.

Exiting the buses, the villagers see that almost nothing remains. Even the well is just a hole in the ground as the stones were taken to re-make it in the fake village half a world away. Only indents in the ground show where their houses once stood. It is quiet as everyone takes in the harsh reality of what has happened to their village.

Home Again

A military vehicle approaches and steps out is Miguel's uncle which is a refreshing and welcome face form the emptiness of the missing village.

Miguel runs to Carlos and hugs him as tears of joy come out of Carlos' eyes.

"It is so good to see you brother," says Manuel coming over to join them.

"You have no idea how much effort I have been putting in to finding you."

Colonel Garza steps forward. "It is true," he says. "He made me believe something was wrong."

"Brother, this is Colonel Garza who is the regional security chief," Carlos says.

"I know you people are exhausted from such a long trip. We have trailers setup fully furnished and with electricity and food – plenty of food. We will resupply you until your homes are rebuilt and life gets back to normal. We are stationed just near that ridge over there in trailers ourselves. Our guys will show you how to use the radio to contact us if you need something. We have patrols to make sure no one comes around here so you can have your peace. We will stay out of your way for the most part. In a couple of days, architects will be here to confer on how to rebuild your homes. Once they are rebuilt we will leave and take these trailers with us. However, because of this incident, the US is paying for a supply

drop to come here regularly giving you food and materials so you may enjoy things a little easier."

"For how long will we get these supplies?" Manuel asks.

"As long as there is a village here," Colonel Garza tells him.

Everyone mumbles in amazement.

"Thank you, Colonel," Manuel says and shakes his hand.

Garza salutes and leaves with his detail. Some of the soldiers show the villagers their trailers and how to use the appliances within.

Carlos looks at Manuel. "Well, this may be too modern for your taste brother."

Manuel looks at Sarah. "I think we will adjust," he says with a smile.

"How is my scientist?" Carlos asks Miguel, smiling down at him.

"I knew where we were," he says with pride.

"Let us go into your trailer and you tell me all about it," Carlos suggests.

They turn into the trailer for an evening of tales of what they went through. The following morning each villager is amazed at

the amount of food that has been left for them. Several soldiers approach as the villagers wander around.

"My name is Sergeant Torres," a soldier introduces himself. "I am here to help you if you have any questions. Your first day with new things you may not be familiar with." At that moment a dust cloud of military vehicles is far away scurrying with a helicopter above them.

"What is going on, Sergeant?" Hector asks.

The sergeant is listening through his earpiece and says, "Sorry, it was a media van trying to drive out here and was stopped. We have orders to let no one near here unless you give permission."

Some villagers ask about how to use the microwave ovens and so forth as Manuel and Carlos walk away.

"You okay, brother?" Carlos asks.

"I am fine. Don't see how things are different than before when the group had us held hostage. We are being watched and isolated just like then."

"I know it is not right. But they are here to protect you, actually."

"Yes, it is just strange."

"It will go back to normal."

"How can it?"

"Trust me it will," Carlos assures him.

"I have had a lot of time to think about it. It will never be the same and maybe that is a good thing. Maybe we need to provide doors for those that want to leave for a different life," says Manuel.

"Well look at you, brother. You are talking about Miguel?"

"Yes. He needs to go to college and be a scientist. He has too much of you in him."

"No, brother, he is all you. The way you used to be," Carlos says.

"You might be right."

They walk quietly. "So are you and Sarah serious about each other?" Carlos asks eventually.

"I asked her to marry me," Manuel says.

Carlos grabs Manuel by the shoulders. "I am so proud, brother. She is beautiful."

"She will never replace Miguel's mother."

"No one can replace a mother but she can be a mother. Let her have that chance," Carlos says.

"She will make a good mother," Manuel admits.

"You are going to be just fine, my brother. I have a confession to make myself. I am engaged."

"What!? You?"

Home Again

Carlos smiles. "Me."

"Who are you marrying?" Manuel asks.

"Remember Eliza?"

"Really? I thought she was already married."

"She was but got an annulment. She was always in love with me and I never knew it."

"That is great news, brother."

The two hug in mutual pride in each other's good fortune.

Days pass as the villagers are becoming accustomed to their new environment and architects arrive to get specifications on homes. Most are quaint and normal in their plans, some want mansions, which eventually are downscaled slightly. Several villagers request to have homes built near towns so they can start a new life there. Manuel and Zane help to guide the rest of the staying villagers to build their future. Zane proves he is a skilled leader and has a lot of good ideas on where things should be.

Eventually, Carlos heads back to his job in town and to Eliza.

Diplomatic

A few weeks after work commences on rebuilding the village a caravan of limousines and police vehicles approach causing everyone to come out to see what was going on. As the line of cars stops several Americans get out and shake hands with the Mexican military officials. Then they approach the villagers.

"Hey everyone, I am Timothy Johnson and I represent the USA. I wanted to say it is good to see you all back in your rightful place and hopefully doing much better after your ordeal. I am here to extend apologies for certain elements, that while not sanctioned by our president, existed within our government's system. Those people are being dealt with harshly. Let me see if there a Miguel and Manuel Ortiz here?"

Listening to the translation, Miguel and Manuel look at each other and step forward. Johnson shakes Manuel's hand. "So good to see you, sir." The Ambassador looks down and shakes Miguel's hand also. "It is a great honor to meet you, young man.

"Mr. Ortiz, the president of the US requests your presence to personally speak with you over this matter – you and your son of course. Look, it is not a commandment," he continues as silence greets his words, "and I know you just started settling back home

but the president would be honored if you would come back with me to visit her. I think you will find it an interesting journey and rewarding. We will have you back here before you know it."

Manual looks down at Miguel as Miguel raises his eyebrows as if to say 'can we?'

"Yes, sir, we will go with you," Manuel says.

"Great, fantastic! We can leave whenever you are ready."

"What about my fiancé Sarah and her daughter?"

Johnson looks at his aide who nods. "Bring them too," he says.

"One hour, sir?" Manuel suggests, seeing Sarah and Laura grinning with delight.

"Certainly, Mr. Ortiz, take your time. I will visit with your fellow villagers while you take care of things."

Manuel walks to Sarah. "Wow, America," he says.

"You have the attention of the president of USA. Such an important man I am marrying." She puts her arms around him as he smiles fondly at her.

"I could get used to this," Manuel says and Sarah laughs and kisses him. They all depart to their trailers to pack their things.

Diplomatic

Meanwhile, Johnson is talking to Hector and Zane. Hector explains how Miguel knew they were not in Mexico anymore. Johnson and his aide listen earnestly as they tell their tale.

"I am glad we all made it back," Hector says.

"Not all of us," Zane points out.

Hector puts his hand on Zane's shoulder.

"I heard about your loss," Johnson says, looking at a report. "That was your mom, right?"

"Yes, sir."

"Well, those responsible for this are facing jail for it. I know nothing can bring her back but we can move forward."

"Thank you, sir."

"Where is Raul?"

"Some people are testing him to make sure he is okay," Hector tells him.

"Good, I was hoping the medical team made it here. They will fix him up," Johnson says.

Miguel, Sarah, Manuel, and Laura walk up with travel bags given them by the soldiers and dressed in new clothes. Johnson claps his hands. "We all ready?" he asks.

"Yes, sir," Manuel replies.

Johnson turns around to the villagers. "It was nice meeting you people and hope to see you again soon."

Manuel and his entourage give hugs and say their goodbyes to the villagers. Hector tells Miguel to 'show them what he is about.'

"You guys live out in the middle of nowhere," the ambassador comments as the limousine pulls away.

"Everywhere is somewhere," Miguel replies.

"Yes, I suppose that's true," Johnson says with a smile.

Miguel and his entourage are quiet the whole trip staring out the windows until eventually, they approach the closest city and airport. The ambassador and his aide are busy discussing itineraries and talking to other officials. As they reach the airplane, they remain quiet just taking everything in, but they know the drill. Miguel makes himself comfortable and looks forward to another plane ride.

The Hammer Falls

News of the abduction keeps preoccupying the media. Most are in praise of Miguel and his ability to discover where they were moved to. People are interviewed on the street saying, “Yeh, we should give those people anything they want. Especially that little boy, he is a hero.”

“I have a little sister if Miguel wants a friend,” a teenage girl tells a reporter. The fandom of their fame continues to spread.

Meanwhile, however, governments are shaken at the implications of the project.

One world leader commented: “This taking of an entire group of people against their will is intolerable. For any government to come in a foreign land and abduct its people all to broker a land deal when no apparent occupants are there, shows an act of war. President Newsome has taken the right action and all the actors in this drama deserve the severest of punishments.”

Several foreign leaders make threats that any military abduction will be met with a military response. President Newsome and her staff watch as threats and posturings are made around the world.

President Newsome calls a fellow president of a powerful country saying, “Thank you, sir, for taking my call. I am sure you are aware of the backlash over the abduction event?”

“Yes, Madam President, you have a lot to clean up. Of course, we will help in any way we can.”

“I think we have it under control. Right now, people that perpetrated this agenda are being arrested. This is a difficult time because of other issues particularly in your area of the world with political relationships being what they are.”

“You just deal with your area and I will keep watch over mine,” the president tells her.

“We will but please know that have a responsibility to take care of those that cannot,” President Newsome says.

“You are a good person, Madam President. We will be in touch.”

“I want updates on all of Violet’s people,” President Newsome tells her staff.

“Yes, Ma’am.”

Destination D.C.

After hours of flying Manuel, Miguel, Sarah and Laura land in Washington D.C. Miguel is excited because he has seen a lot of buildings and interesting places through the plane's windows. Limousines pick them up at the airport and drive to the Whitehouse. They all follow the Ambassador as he tells them facts about what they are seeing. It almost seems like background noise as their attention is visual, taking it all in.

"Yes, Ambassador, I was informed to let the president know as soon as you guys arrive. Do they require anything after a long trip?" the president's secretary asks.

"I think they are okay, they were taken care of on the flight."

The secretary gets on the phone and shortly a man appears who is the press secretary.

"Hi, everyone, I am press secretary Henry Tucker and we are about to see the president. I just wanted to go over a few things before we go in. First off there is going to be camera people in there, don't let them bother you. Just be yourself, they will be using the best photos of you for publicity. When we go in there, I will introduce you to the president and she will likely shake your hand as I introduce each one of you. We will all sit on the couches

and she will ask you questions. Just again be yourself don't be afraid. She is very friendly and this is supposed to be a pleasant visit. Everyone understand? Questions?"

Miguel shrugs his shoulder as they hear the translation and Tucker walk them into the Oval Office.

"Madam President, may I introduce Manuel, Miguel, Sarah, and Laura. Guys this is President Vickie Newsome."

"It is so nice to meet you, fine people," Vickie says as she walks over to shake their hands. She turns to the Ambassador. "Hi, Tim, how are you?"

"I am good, Madam President."

Tucker holds a hand out indicating to have a seat as they all sit on the couches facing each other. Manuel and his people on one couch while the Press Secretary and Ambassador sit on the other while Vickie sits in a chair between them.

"Well then, what a tale you people have lived."

Manuel turns to Sarah and smiles but they say nothing.

Vickie looks at the Ambassador as he smiles back.

"You know," Vickie continues, "when I heard about what happened, I was simply stunned and even angry. I wondered who could have done this and then learned it was an old nemesis by the

name of Violet. I thought I had effectively dealt with her long ago but seems she wielded some power without my knowledge. However, this is being remedied."

Still, silence as none of the visitors know what to say. Vickie looks at the floor and thinks for a moment. "You know what, let's get out of here."

"Ma'am, where would you like to go?"

"Get the helicopter ready, we are going for a ride."

"Where to, ma'am?" one official asks.

"Up and around town to show them the sights." The secret service man calls out to get Marine One ready. Vickie walks up to Miguel and Laura and kneels down. "How would like to see the city from the air?" Their eyes light up as they nod. Vickie smiles. "Awesome."

They are escorted to the lawn as the helicopter arrives. As it lifts off Vickie describes the monuments they are seeing. They get a tour of the Pentagon and the whole city as the helicopter flies around. Vickie looks at Miguel. "I know what you want to see," she says. "Take us to the Naval Observatory," she tells the pilot.

The helicopter approaches and Miguel's eyes light up, as he knows what an observatory looks like.

"Father, it is a telescope," Miguel says.

"Where, son?" Manuel says, looking around.

"Inside the round building."

The helicopter lands as security are already in place to receive them. As they enter the building a lady in a lab-coat is waiting. "Hi mom," she says, hugging Vickie.

"Everybody, this is the scientist in charge of special projects at this observatory, my daughter, Veronica. Veronica this is Miguel the young man I told you about and his father Manuel, friends Sarah and Laura." Veronica shakes their hands. "I hear you are quite an astronomer," she says to Miguel.

"I want to be."

"Really? Well, tell me, what is the best-known constellation that we would see here if it was night right now."

Miguel thinks about it. "Orion," he says.

Veronica smiles. "Very good, you are an astronomer." Then looks at Laura; "What do you think?"

Laura looks up at her mom. "I think I am going to have the best brother ever."

"Brother?" Veronica says.

"My mom and his dad are getting married."

"Well congratulations, you guys."

"Thank you," Sarah says.

"That is exciting," says Vickie. "When are you getting married?"

Manuel and Sarah look at each other. "Well we have not set a date yet," Sarah says.

"Well I tell you what, you tell me when and where you would like your wedding and I will bring you and your entire village to it and pay for it myself. I will also send you on a honeymoon anywhere you like."

"Thank you, Ma'am president. You are very kind," Manuel says.

"It is my pleasure. Now, how about we get this boy to that observatory?"

Veronica escorts them as she explains the history of the observatory and walks them through displays until they reach the actual main night visual telescope.

"Quite a sight, isn't it?" Veronica says, seeing Miguel's eyes fixed on it.

"It is beautiful. Father, isn't that great?"

"It is something son," Manuel agrees.

"Well, we don't use the telescope anymore, it is more a tourist attraction, but we do maintain others in other places. These facilities do many other important things now."

Veronica takes Miguel and Laura to see the workings of the telescope as Vickie stays with Manuel and Sarah.

"Mr. Ortiz, you have a gifted son there," Vickie says.

"I am proud of him. He has always had such a love of the stars. He stays up all night at times just staring at them."

"It would be a shame if he did not go to college and do something with that interest."

"I know, he deserves it. He certainly is not cut out to be a goat herder or farmer."

"Nothing wrong with any of that but for Miguel, it is astronomy. You know I have an idea."

"Yes, ma'am?"

"How about we send a tutor to help him and the rest of your villagers with school. It will prepare Miguel for college."

"We have a tutor that comes out once in a while to help the kids," Manuel says.

"Yes, but I am talking about full-time school and we will focus on Miguel and anyone else that has interest in something."

"He would love that, but how can I pay for college?"

"I will."

"Ma'am?"

"I will pay all his college fees and Laura's too. Also, anyone else that wants it in your village. But Miguel will go to the finest

university for astronomy and then will intern with my daughter Veronica during and after college. That means he will have a job doing what he loves."

"You would do that for us?" Sarah says.

Vickie smiles. "Yes, of course."

Sarah looks at Manuel as he looks at the ground and then back to Sarah. "I don't know how to thank you," he says.

"So, it is a deal?" Vickie asks.

"Whatever Miguel wants to do."

Sarah hugs Manuel. "I am proud of you and Sofia would be too."

"I know," Manuel says.

Vickie looks confused but then realizes Sofia must be Manuel's late wife.

"It is settled then," Vickie says. They all look on as Miguel and Laura are talking to Veronica and asking a million questions. Veronica looks back and smiles at them.

Manuel and Sarah go by themselves to look at some displays and have time to themselves.

"It has all happened so quickly. How can I go back to the old life?" Manuel asks.

"Who says it has to be the old life for any of us?" Sarah says. "They are giving us homes, electricity, appliances, and supplies.

All we have to do is what we love to do. If it means raising crops and animals, that is what we do. We just live a little better but never leave who we are. Also, it is a chance to not be prisoners of a life that is hard just because some of us feel guilty." Manuel looks at her with a confused look as she continues. "You know what I am talking about, Mr. Ortiz set yourself free. You deserve to be happy and live again to sing and be who you want to be."

Manuel stares in silence and then smiles. "I am going to marry you as soon as possible," he tells Sarah. "What could I possibly give you that is better than all we have just been given?"

Sarah laughs. "A child of our own?"

Manuel smiles as a secret service man following far behind catches up. "Sir, Ma'am we are ready to go now." They follow him back as Miguel and Laura are waiting with Vickie and Veronica.

"Well son, did you get an eyeful?" Manuel asks.

Miguel grins. "Oh yes, sir."

They leave on Marine One back to the White House for pictures in the Oval Office. After the posing for pictures Vickie says, "Folks, please stay here as long as you like as our guest and my people will tour you around anywhere you want to be in our fine country."

"That would be fun," Manuel says.

"Good. That's a deal. Before you leave I have some presents for Laura and Miguel. Here you go little miss," Vickie says and Laura a parcel. Laura opens it to find a music jewelry box with necklaces in it. Her eyes light up as she shows her mom. Vickie is handed another box and kneels down to Miguel and says, "For you, sir."

Miguel stares at the box and looks at his dad as Manuel nods to open it. Miguel in anticipation slowly opens the box pulling out a grey rock encased in plastic. "Ma'am, what is this?" he asks.

"That is a rock from the moon. Only a handful of people outside our government possess any. Now you are one of them," Vickie tells him.

"Wow, a rock from the moon. Thank you, Ma'am President."

Vickie hands Miguel a device and says, "This is for you too, just in case you find yourself again where you should not be."

Miguel looks confused again. "What is this, ma'am?"

"It is a satellite phone and it is programmed to call me directly. You ever need me, you call me anytime. It will ring directly to my cell phone. My people will show you how to use it, okay?"

Miguel looks at the phone and quickly hugs Vickie. "Okay," Vickie says and stands up. "I mean it, Miguel, you can call me anytime."

"Yes, Ma'am President."

They leave waving as they are taken to a nice hotel to rest and decide where to go next. Upon Manuel asking them where they should go next to the kids immediately want to go to a theme park.

"And just how do you know there is such a thing as a theme park?" Manuel asks.

"You don't know about theme parks?" Laura says, aghast.

Miguel looks at Sarah as she gives a sign to Manuel to stop torturing the kids.

"Okay, theme park it is," Manuel says.

Emancipation Vacation

They travel to a state of sunshine where tourism thrives. After they settle in Miguel and Laura are awestruck by the splendor of a theme park that never seems to end. Their enthusiasm is unbridled wanting to try everything. Their handlers have ensured easy, quick access past the mass of crowds. Yet everyone knows who they are and have no issue surrendering their place in line to rides to accommodate the villagers. Sometimes they are applauded and asked to stop to have their pictures taken. It is a time they will never forget and as the day drones on the kids begin to be tired, their excitement draining away. They head back to the hotel and are delivered a good meal to finish the day. Manuel and Sarah look at the TV and stations that seem endless. Everything seems geared to end any boredom yet they are bored of it all already. However, they must play it out for their children's benefit.

The following day the family returns to the theme park but, although Miguel and Laura still enjoy the rides, they are less excited than the day before and by lunchtime ask to leave. Their guides take them on a tour of historical sites and around the

country. After days of touring the end up in a beautiful desert area that seems painted with many colors.

"Laura, where is Miguel?" Manuel asks as night draws in.

"He is sitting on a rock looking at the stars."

Manuel walks over to Miguel. "What is wrong, son?"

"Nothing, sir."

"You miss home, don't you?"

"I've had fun here but, yes, I miss home," Miguel admits.

"We have to go back to the US president one last time and then they will send us home. We will go back tomorrow."

"Dad…"

"Yes, son."

"Do you think it is silly for a farm boy to want to be an astronomer?"

"I think it is the greatest thing in the world for a farm boy to become an astronomer," Manuel tells him.

"People here are raised to be clever and study things like astronomy. I am way behind."

Manuel puts his arm around his son. "Miguel, did they figure out we were in the wrong part of the world? Have they the enthusiasm to watch the stars almost every night? I don't think so.

You see, son, sometimes what seems like an advantage can prove to hold people back. It is the starving person that savors the food more. You have a hunger and a mind that is made for stars. You will be one of the greats."

Miguel smiles. "Thank you, Dad. Can we go home now?"

"Let's go home."

They head back to their hotel as Manuel informs the guides they are done with the tour. Preparations are made to head back to Washington D.C. and the president is informed.

"Good, I was ready to go home," Sarah says as Manuel informs her of their decision. "How about you, little girl?"

Laura looks up. "I guess so. Although I did like that theme park."

"Maybe you will go back there someday," Sarah says.

The next morning the plane flies them back to Washington and they meet the president one last time.

"You guys find a good place for your wedding and honeymoon?" Vickie asks.

"Well, we talked about it on the plane and actually we would like to be married in our village."

"I am not sure about the honeymoon," Manuel adds, "we are still thinking about it."

"Well, that sounds like a good thing. I have something for you, Mr. Ortiz," Vickie says.

"Yes, Madam President?"

"Do you know the name, Martin De Lopez?"

"Oh yes, he is a music legend in my country."

"Well, all over, actually. I spoke with him and told him you used to be a singer. He wants to cut an album with you."

Manuel turns around as everyone stares at each other in silence. "That is a dream come true for me."

"When you get settled back home, call him. My people have his information for you," Vickie says.

"Thank you, Madam President."

"You are welcome, sir." Vickie looks down at Miguel. "You still have that phone?"

"Yes, ma'am."

"Good."

"Ma'am, what is going to happen to Ms. Chambers?" Miguel asks.

Vickie looks at her staff who remind her of Jill Chambers and the Senate hearings. Vickie replies, "Oh, Miguel she is facing charges with the others for her part in your abduction."

Miguel stares at the ground. “Does she have to? She helped us.”

“Well she was not innocent, she was a part of it too,” Vickie says.

“I don’t want this phone if she is going to jail,” Miguel says holding out the phone.

Vickie is taken aback and pushes the phone back to him. “Keep the phone, I will pardon Ms. Chambers. She will not go to jail, deal?”

Miguel’s eyes light up. “Deal.”

Vickie smiles. “Guys, I must cut this short as I have a crisis to deal with. Seems some kind of virus outbreak is occurring in Europe. It is always something but I wish you all pleasant journey home and thank you for seeing me again.”

They all pose for photos for the press before making their way back home to Mexico.

It Is Good To Be Back

They arrive home at the village houses have been finished and the trailers have been moved away. There is only a small contingent of government officials living nearby to make sure no one outside the village bothers them. The villagers come out and hug as they are excited to see the weary travelers.

"The place has not been the same without you, but we have been watching you on the TV," Hector says.

"It is good to be back. It was nice to see those places but this is home. Even Miguel was ready to come back."

"Well, the boy is growing up then."

"This is where the stars are always right," Miguel says with a smile.

Everyone in the village laughs. "And we are thankful for that," Hector says slapping him on the back.

"I see they finished the homes," Manuel says.

"Oh yes, we even have electricity and running water. They also ran water to the animal pens and farm area."

"What about the rest of you? Anyone traveling?" Manuel asks.

"Some of the young people want to but we're looking forward to hearing about your trip first," Hector tells him.

"Well, there are a lot of nice places to visit and things to see. But home is home as far as I am concerned," Manuel tells the crowd.

Manuel looks over to a slab of concrete set a little way off from the village. "What is that?" he asks.

"Not sure, it is something they are building they said we need. Said they would be back to finish it when materials come in," Hector tells him.

Sarah gives Hector a big hug. "How are you?" she asks.

"I am fine. Look what they have given me."

Hector takes Sarah to his house and behind is a pen with a beautiful black horse. "Now what gave them the idea to give me a horse?" he asks her with a smile.

"I guess they know everything. Are you able to ride it?" Sarah says.

"Zane helps me and, yes, I have ridden Shadowlove a few times."

Sarah grins. "I am glad." She leaves him to catch up with Manuel.

It Is Good To Be Back

Manuel and Miguel arrive in their new home and are amazed that they have modern appliances and even a TV, yet it was designed with a rustic charm to remind them of their old home.

"What do you think, Dad?"

"You know I could get used to it."

They both laugh as they hear a knock on the door. Miguel invites Sarah and Laura in to look around.

"Very nice but could use a woman's touch," Sarah remarks.

"What about your home?" Manuel asks.

"It is beautiful," Sarah says.

"Sounds like we will have a hard time picking which one to live in."

"Not hard at all. Wherever you are is where I want to live."

"I think they anticipated it when building this house because it has four bedrooms," Manuel says.

"Four?"

"Yes, one for us, one each for the kids and one nursery."

Sarah grabs Manuel by the head and kisses him. "My man."

Miguel and Laura look at each other before going to look at their new rooms.

"I love you, Manuel," Sarah says.

"You have brought love back into my heart, Sarah," Manuel tells her.

As they hug they laugh, hearing Miguel and Laura argue on which room will be the nursery and which one Laura's.

"Should we break this up?" Manuel asks.

"Let's just hold each other and listen to it," Sarah says, snuggling closer.

The following day Manuel wakes to smell food cooking.

"Good morning," Manuel says, entering the kitchen to find Sarah cooking breakfast.

"Good morning to you, sir," Sarah replies.

"Hmmm, smells good."

There is a knock on the door and Manuel opens it to find Carlos.

"Brother!" they say simultaneously and embrace.

"Eliza, it is so good to see you again," Manuel says, spotting her standing behind Carlos.

"You too, Manuel," Eliza says with a smile.

"I like the new place brother," says Carlos.

Miguel runs and grabs Carlos. "Uncle!"

"Well look at the world traveler," Carlos says with a smile.

It Is Good To Be Back

"Come sit at the table and let's enjoy some of this good breakfast Sarah is preparing," Manuel says.

"Hi, Sarah, nice to see you again. You know Eliza?"

"Hello, Carlos, and it is so good to see you again Eliza. How do you like your eggs?"

"Like any man, scrambled of course," Carlos replies.

Sarah laughs. "Of course. And you, Eliza?"

"Let me help you with that," Eliza offers and moves to join Sarah at the stove.

"Well, how has it been?" Manuel asks his brother as they sit at the table.

"Like we spoke last time, it still amazes me the adventure you people went through."

"Some adventure. More like a nightmare."

"I am sure it was, especially when you realized you were not home," Carlos says.

Sarah and Eliza bring over plates of food. "I got to wake up my little girl and bring her over, be right back," Sarah says.

"Let me come with you," says Eliza who follows her out of the house.

"Uncle, you know you saved us by helping me understand the stars?" Miguel says.

Carlos and Manuel look at each other. “Well I may have started you on the path but you heard the call. It is all, you Miguel. You figured it out and took action,” Carlos tells him

Miguel smiles and keeps eating.

“I know you told me before, but you really had the government concerned right?” Manuel says.

“Oh yes, once I got them to listen, they were all over it. But not knowing where you were, the leads went cold. However, I think they suspected quite a bit.”

“Did you get any media bothering you about it?”

“Oh yes, they hounded my home for weeks. Especially every time you popped up on the news traveling around the USA. Everyone traveled with you in their hearts.”

“It was a nice place,” Manuel admits, “but this is home. It was Miguel that made the call to come back.”

“Really?”

“I felt like coming back,” Miguel says.

“You are growing up,” Carlos says with a smile.

“Brother, let me ask you this. What are they building near the village?” Manuel asks.

"It is water tower so that pumped in water can be stored," Carlos tells him.

"Oh okay. I guess that makes sense in case of drought."

"Uncle, Dad is going to make a song with De Lopez," Miguel says.

"*The* De Lopez?" Carlos says.

"Yes, the American president arranged it. We are going to make an album together," Manuel tells him.

"That is incredible, brother."

"I have always wanted to make a record since I was young. Just hope I can do okay."

"You will be fine. They will help you through it," Carlos says.

Sarah and Eliza walk in with Laura

"Manners, little miss," Sarah says as Laura jumps up to the table and immediately eats. Laura ignores her and keeps eating. Eliza winks at Carlos who returns her smile.

"I am going to dedicate the album to my new family," Manuel announces.

"Thanks, Dad," says Miguel.

"Album?" asks Eliza.

"My brother is going to make an album with De Lopez," Carlos tells her.

"*The* De Lopez!"

"Hopefully I won't embarrass him," Manuel says.

“What you going to name the album, then?” Carlos asks between mouthfuls of food.

“Well, I guess that would be up to De Lopez, but if they ask I think maybe –”

Sarah interrupts. “Sofia!”

Manuel and Miguel stare at her. “What?” says Manuel.

“It should be named after Sofia because you and she sang together and she would be honored by it.”

Manuel grabs Sarah’s hand and looks at Carlos. “She is the finest woman I could ask for. Just like Eliza is as well of course.”

“Well, we are men of untold wealth, brother. What do you think, nephew?” Carlos says.

“Miss Martinez is the mother I always hoped to have. It makes me very happy to have her as my mom and Laura as my sister. I think the album should be named Sofia as she said. That way when the album is played by many she can sing in the heavens and remember.”

Manuel sits stunned. “Son, it will be named Sofia, I promise you.” He looks up at Sarah. “But I am still dedicating it to you, my love.”

Sarah smiles. “I love you,” she says.

It Is Good To Be Back

Miguel runs to his room and comes back with a box. "Here, uncle, I want you to have this. It was a present from the American president."

Carlos opens the box. "What is it?" he asks.

"It is a moon rock."

"That is a gem for sure. However, I think it belongs to you. Thank you, though, nephew."

"You can borrow it if you like," Miguel offers.

"You know what? I will come and look at it when I visit. I would hate to lose it or have it stolen. It is too valuable."

Carlos and Eliza stay for two days. Sarah and Eliza spend their time together like sisters as Sarah shows her how to sew.

"I have always wanted to learn this but never did," Eliza tells her.

"I enjoy it," Sarah says. "There is something peaceful about making things. It is a practical hobby."

"It is really nice being here, so quiet. No cars or sirens like the city. I have to admit the new homes are much more comfortable than your old ones."

"That's for sure," Sarah admits with a laugh. "It was not bad before though, you can get used to anything. You just have to accept your life as it is and then happiness will follow."

"That is a very nice way of putting it. I hope we come back here to visit often."

"Well, you are always welcome."

"Thank you. So, tell me what do you have planned for your wedding?"

"The American president offered us something nice but I think we will keep it simple. What about you?"

"You know I don't know. Maybe have it here," Eliza says.

"Here? You sure?"

"Why not?"

"I figured you city people would do something in the city," Sarah says.

"I have no family in the city. I think there would be appropriate."

"That is nice."

"You know Carlos was going nuts trying to find you," Eliza says.

"Well, we would have never made it back if it hadn't been for Miguel."

"You think they would have done something bad to you all?" Eliza asks her.

"Yes. There was no way to bring us back. We were proof of their plans and they had already killed one of us."

"Very scary."

"Yes, but God was watching over us," Sarah says.

"With the help of a little boy."

"Yes, I will be proud to call him son soon."

The time came eventually to depart.

Carlos looks at Miguel. "Before I leave I have something for you," he says and goes to his jeep and pulls out a box. Miguel opens the box with anticipation and pulls out a key.

"What is this key for, uncle?" he asks.

"You will see. Keep it safe," Carlos says.

"Okay, I will."

Miguel gives Carlos and Eliza a hug and waves them off.

The Bells Ring the Valley

Months pass and the big day has arrived – a beautiful day for Manuel's and Sarah's wedding. The village has transformed into a gala event with the heads of the Mexican government and military attending and US president Vickie and her daughter Veronica. Some of the Australian military and police that helped rescue the villagers are also witnessing the event. TV is covering the event and De Lopez is there to play music from his new number one hit album 'Sofia'.

Carlos, the best man, and Manuel stand at the altar waiting for Sarah and Miguel and Laura carry rings down the aisle before standing aside, smiling.

"What are you so nervous about? You have been through this before," Carlos whispers.

"Not with the world watching and with world leaders at my wedding."

"Don't worry about that. It is just you and Sarah today." Carlos smiles at Eliza who blows him a kiss.

"Did you and Eliza build the archway here?"

"No, Zane and Donkey did," Carlos says.

Manuel looks at Zane and Raul and nods as they smile back.

“You know…” Manuel says, at that moment glimpsing Sarah standing at the end of the aisle. She is stunning in her dress, looking like a doll.

“Oh brother,” Carlos says.

“Sofia, forgive me, but she is the most beautiful thing I have ever seen,” Manuel says.

“I think Sofia is agreeing with you,” Carlos tells him.

The priest calls everyone to attention and, as he reads passages and observations, the sound of his voice fades for Manuel and Sarah as they stare at each other. They hear only the subtle and warm whisper of desert wind covering them like a loving blanket. Nothing matters at this moment but their love for each other. Miguel and Laura hold hands knowing they will become siblings soon. Time seems to slow down as the moment lasts forever. The ceremony proceeds with no issue and the priest announces them as man and wife. They kiss as the world cheers.

At the reception in the evening, De Lopez sings as Vickie and other government dignitaries approach Manuel and Sarah to say congratulations before they go.

“Where did you two decide to go on your honeymoon?” Vickie asks.

The Bells Ring The Valley

"We are going to hear my husband sing with De Lopez on stage in Mexico City then pick up the kids who will be with Carlos."

"That sounds like a nice getaway," Vickie says. "Oh, by the way, the Australian government erected a monument to your village at the site where you were abducted to. Here is a picture of it." Her aide hands the picture to her and she gives it to Hector.

Vickie and officials depart, but first Vickie approaches Miguel. "Every astronomer needs a telescope, don't you think? Even if it is something simple to start them off. My daughter is picking one out for you and should be here soon. I hope you enjoy it."

"Thank you, ma'am," Miguel says.

Manuel and Sarah depart for their honeymoon while Carlos and Eliza take their kids to their new place in the city. As Laura and Miguel place their belongings in Carlos' vehicle he says to Miguel, "Migs, go over to that group of people there." Miguel looks at them and back at his uncle in confusion but heads over there anyway. The men move out of Miguel's way revealing Jill Chambers. She kneels down to hug him.

"How are you, little man?" Jill says.

"I am so glad you are not in jail."

“Me too. Your plea to the president got me a pardon and I will not go to jail. Matter of fact I have a job working for the president’s science team now.

“I am so happy.”

“I have a gift for you,” Jill says and reaches into her purse and pulls out a piece of metal rod.

“What is this?” Miguel asks.

“I had to pull some strings in my new job but I acquired this for you. It is a piece of the last space shuttle that flew for America. You have a part of a vehicle that went into space. It is a part of history now.”

“Wow, thank you.” Miguel’s eyes boggle as he stares at the metal rod.

“I have to get back but I wanted to see you. I will come back and visit you from time to time.”

“Promise?”

Jill smiles through her tears. “It’s a promise.”

They hug as she leaves with the others in her group.

Miguel waves as they leave and walks to Carlos, Eliza and Laura showing them what she gave him.

The Valley

“Looks like a pipe,” Laura says with a frown. Miguel gives a smirk as Carlos laughs. Eliza puts Laura in the jeep.

“Alright guys, let’s head out,” Carlos says.

Equinox

After the honeymoon, Carlos and Eliza bring Miguel and Laura back to the village from the city. Manuel describes the concert to the villagers with a sparkle in his eye, as Sarah looks on with pride. The villagers laugh and pay full attention as Manuel shows the signed guitar DeLopez gave him.

"He told me he will tour with me from time to time," Manuel tells them.

"Do you really want to embrace the modern world like that, Manuel?" Hector asks.

Manuel looks to the ground and chuckles. "This will always be home to me no matter what. I am not leaving here, but I see nothing wrong with a vacation once in a while."

"I will take care of things for you when you are gone, my man," Zane tells him.

"Thank you, Zane. I can't think of a better man to run this place when I am away."

"Think I will go wander around and see if I can find any more strange buildings," Raul says.

"Didn't you learn the first time? Just stick around here," Zane tells him.

“Okay.” Raul laughs and brays as everyone chuckles.

“As for you, young man,” Manuel says looking at Miguel, “you have a lot of learning to do if you are going away to college.”

“Yes, sir.”

“I see you made a necklace out of that key I gave you,” Carlos says.

Miguel looks down and smiles. “Yes, sir. It always stays with me.”

“We have set a date for our wedding,” Eliza tells them. One year from the anniversary of your wedding. We want it to be an equally special day for all of us.”

Life is good for the villagers as they enjoy some comforts of the modern world but without the ties that make debtors out of many of us. For it seems nothing is wrong with a few conveniences if they do not become the sole pursuit of one’s life. Their economy stays simple, lives fulfilled and they continue to work hard and stress only about what matters. Their trial and unjust abduction have been well compensated and they live as they once did – well with a few exceptions. They now have the best of both worlds. We should be so lucky.

Equinox

Evening has descended and the whole village waits outside for Carlos, Eliza, Manuel and his new family.

"How do the stars look?" they ask Miguel who looks up and replies, "They are perfect."

"I think that some stars we see may actually be farther away than we think," Raul observes.

"What makes you think that, Donkey?" Carlos says.

Eliza slaps Carlos and smiles. "Raul," she says.

"Sorry, Raul." Manuel smiles shaking his head at Carlos.

Raul looks around. "You know how the sun seems bigger at times. Something in the air plays tricks with our eyes and changes their size. You know like a magnifying glass."

The villagers all turn to Raul and stare in amazement as Miguel smiles at him.

Raul looks at everyone. "What?" he asks.

Carlos puts his arm around Raul. "You know, Raul, you are a smart man."

Miguel pats Raul as he looks at his dad.

"I guess you are going to look at the stars?" Manuel says.

"Yes, sir."

"Well, don't stay up too late."

Miguel smiles as he walks up to new building built near the village. It is his observatory and has the telescope Vickie promised

him – a large reflector telescope that would make any professional astronomer happy. Miguel unlocks it with his key and smiles at the plaque next to the door that says: ‘Miguel’s’.

Epilogue

From the hardcover jacket:

Vickie is a character from the so-named series of books also by Mike Sims. Vickie is a strong female character that handles many real-life issues. They are adult subject books but Mike felt compelled to borrow Vickie in Southern Cross. In this book he shares a rare glimpse into her character and issue she faces not written about much in her series of books.

Violet is another character borrowed from the Vickie series of books by Mike Sims. Violet is a strong and financially powerful woman who is the nemesis to Vickie. While she is implied in Southern Cross, we get to witness her influence. In the Vickie

series, she is a key character Vickie must deal with. Mike used Violet to cross-pollinate this book with the Vickie series.

Southern Cross is an adventure story that demonstrates the importance of education and understanding about the world. Miguel is a boy of modest living but dreams big and keeps looking up.

Southern Cross came from a short story Mike wrote many years ago and shared with close friends and family it became a favorite among them. Taking time from writing his Vickie series, he wanted to bring this short story to novel. Southern Cross is an all age story and one of the author's favorites in his collection of short

stories. He hopes you will enjoy Southern Cross as much as he did writing it.

Epilogue

A note from the author:

I hope you enjoyed Southern Cross. It is one of my most popular and favorite short stories from my collection of many. As many short stories, they often come in dreams or daydreams that just pops into my head. I jot them down quickly and then work on it later as time permits. My collection of short stories went on for many years however I never felt I had what it takes to write an actual novel even though family and friends encouraged me to. It wasn't until about 2004 when I entered a writing contest of thousands of entries for a short story. The story I entered was one of my horror stories that fit their criteria. To my surprise, I won 4th place. I believed that I had something to offer but still did not pursue it. The following year after starting a new job an idea for a dark comedy popped in my head about a man that assaults a woman named Vickie. She revenges herself upon him over many years in bizarre ways. As I wrote it, the story turned dramatic and

ended much different than I first anticipated. After putting it down in words I realized it was too big for a short story. I did not understand what to do with it so it sat for 8 years. In 2012 following the death of my boss the story came how to write it. I worked on it for two years in three drafts. My wife went through correcting things and then my good friend Nicole worked on it. Then she had her mom go through it who is a retired literary professor. Then finally her aunt who is a literary major combed through it. Passing through those editorial gauntlets I sent this "masterpiece" to literary agents. Having been turned down by all 500 I submitted it to second tier publishers. These publishers do not require agents but sometimes they are more publishing services than publishing houses. However after four months I self-published it and checked it off my bucket list of things accomplished. Then a vanity publisher offered to publish my book. Their reputation was not very good but it was a quantum

leap from where I was. So I came to an agreement and they published my book Vic/Tim. It was exciting and they treated me well. That was until I received no royalties after writing two more novels Vickie and Valkyrie as a series to Vic/Tim. So I moved away from my publisher and struck it out on my own. At this time I already knew enough to publish on my own in many formats.

I am still working on the Vickie book series now translated in many languages and even in audiobook form. I have been fortunate that my book Vickie was narrated by a movie actress and she loved the story so much, she showed it to a producer. Now it is being vetted for a TV movie or series. Meanwhile Southern Cross continues my venture in writing books and is the first non-traditional publisher book I have produced. So thank you for reading my book and I hope you follow me along my journey.

Mike Sims

www.Mazzaroth.net

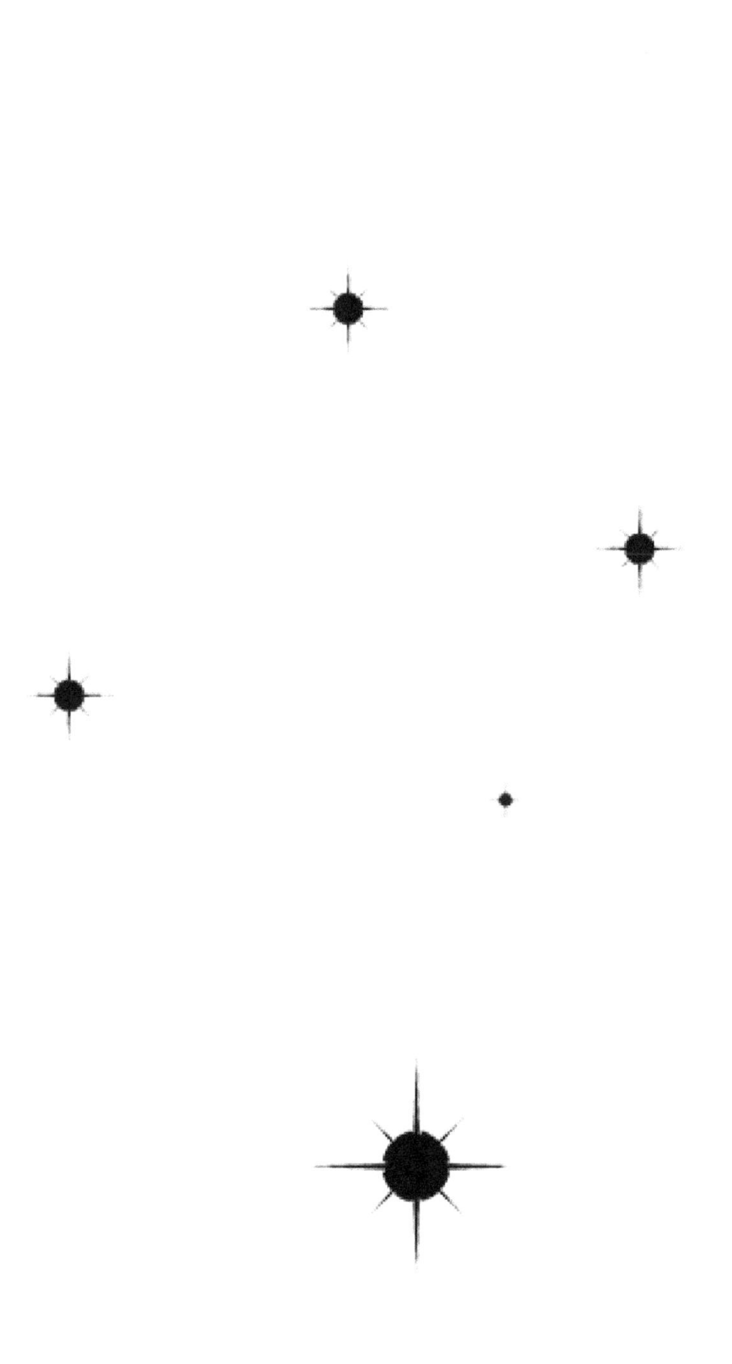

www.ingramcontent.com/pod-product-compliance
Lightning Source LLC
Chambersburg PA
CBHW060550310726
48982CB00008B/1071/J
9780998298399